Promiseland

By
Dawn Miller

INTEGRITY®
PUBLISHERS
Nashville

Library of Congress Cataloging-in-Publication Data

Miller, Dawn.
    Promiseland : the journal of Callie McGregor / by Dawn Miller.
      p. cm.
    ISBN 1-59145-001-2
      1. Women pioneers—Fiction.   2. Montana—Fiction.   I. Title.

PS3563.I376715 P76 2002
813'.54–dc21

                                                    2002068544

Printed in the United States of America
02 03 04 05 06 LBM 9 8 7 6 5 4 3 2 1

This book is dedicated to You, Lord, for lighting my way home . . .

PART ONE

Going to the Promiseland

Mama,
Pa and me bot this jernal for you in
Virgenya Sity so you culd rite in it.
Uncl Jack says we are goin to our
promisland. Pa red me the story about
Moses so I wrote on the next page to
and Pa said that is good enuff.
Love,
Rose

Then Moses liftd his arm and God said,
"Go forth and dont be scairt, IM with
the to make sur you git there."

By Rose McGregor
age 9
Mountana Teritery, 1869

Near the Yellowstone River
Montana Territory
August 30, 1869 . . .

My mama used to say life ain't measured by the breaths we take but by the times that take our breath away . . . This land, this bold stretch of mountain valley Jack calls our "promiseland," takes my breath away. Only I'm not sure if that's good or bad or if I'll ever be able to catch my breath again . . .

We are a day yet from the new homestead, and so many thoughts and feelings flood my mind . . . so many memories. I guess if ever there was a good time for memories, this would be it. When I look out across camp at the other wagons, hearing the bawl of cattle, the snap and pop of a dying fire mingling with the sighs of my Rose and Patrick as they sleep, it's hard not to think of memories of another time . . . of family, of where we've come from or where we're going. And to hope that maybe we're almost through the wilderness that's been our lives.

Drifters—that's what our old preacher back home would call us. *"If you kids don't learn to sit still now,"* he'd say, *"you'll turn to drifters later, mark my words . . ."*

Seeing the tired, dust-smudged faces of my brother, Jack, and his new wife, Lillie, . . . of our old friend Stem and his Jessie . . . of Coy Harper, . . . even my Quinn tonight, I can't help thinking how we *have* all been a bit like drifters, scattered to the wind, not sure where we'd land next—or if we would. But we have a hope now in us, too.

And hope, like the Good Book says, is the anchor of the soul.

If ever there was a family that needed an anchor, it's us.

I can't seem to find the right words to describe how it feels for us all to be a family again, to have Jack back with us. Maybe because I feared so long that I wouldn't—see Jack alive again, I mean. Mama always believed he'd make it, though.

I was half-listening to the men talking at dinner tonight when a memory came to me of when I was just a girl, standing with Mama on the front porch of our farm back in Missouri as we looked together across the field Pa had just plowed for Jack. I remember being mad at Jack for running out on the chores, and I had mumbled that he'd probably lit out for good with the cardsharps he'd been running with. Mama had just looked at me then with a look that wasn't angry—just kind of sad—like I hadn't caught on to what was important.

"Jack's got good in him, Callie," she'd said. "He just doesn't believe it yet. That's what the good Lord puts families together for, to believe in each other when we can't believe in ourselves." Then she just smiled easy and said, "Your brother will be back. Our hearts always lead us home . . ."

Like most everything else she told me, she was right about Jack—he came back—and watching him from across the campfire this evening, smiling with Lillie as he held his little boy on his knee, I saw the man he was becoming.

"You just mark my words down in that little journal of yours, Callie," he said to me. "We're gonna be cattle pioneers, sure enough."

"We'll see," I said, grinning in spite of trying not to.

"You just wait," Jack chuckled. "Come next spring you'll be eating crow."

Everyone laughed at that. Crow has always been a tough bird for me to chew—especially when Jack's the one serving it.

"Almost like old times, wouldn't ya say, lass?" Quinn said, smiling, his blue eyes crinkling at the corners. I couldn't help thinking if it weren't for those crinkles, it *could've* been old times. Could have been all of us as we once were, when we'd all started out to find our home in the West.

Stem's here, just like he was that first day, as our scout: a thin, wiry old mulatto dressed in buckskins who took my hand and told us he'd be leading us west . . . and I remembered my sister saying how he looked like her Bible pictures of Moses, "*'cept for that wooden leg of his,*" she'd added with relish, like Moses should've had a wooden leg, too.

Stem leaned over then and whispered something in Jessie's ear, and as I watched her laugh, her dark face wreathed in a smile, I remembered the day she'd tromped past our wagon train. Folks had whispered she was a *runaway slave*. Stem liked to say he and Jessie had been "weathered" by life. I can't help thinking we've all been weathered by life since that first day . . .

Quinn wasn't my husband yet, but he stood by me, always willing to carry my burden as we buried my pa and sister along the trail . . . and again, when Jack had rode away from us, so heartbroken. And Jack hadn't yet married a Blackfoot woman—Raven was her name, and they had a child together—only to see her murdered before his and their son John-Charles's eyes—hadn't yet met Lillie, who'd become his wife and mama to John-Charles. And Coy, the mighty black oak that refused to topple even after traveling mile after mile to find his pa, only to learn he had been killed trying to save Jack . . .

Sometimes it doesn't seem possible to me that we all made it through alive—or "alive and kickin' back," as Stem likes to say. Seems downright *impossible.* But we're alive and together again—an answer to the months and months of prayers I wouldn't quit. Or maybe couldn't . . .

"You always believed," Quinn whispered to me last night as we lay in the wagon together . . . Sometimes I wonder if he knows how those prayers kept me alive as much as they did Jack. How I clung to them like a lifeline, searching for some sign of land, for somewhere we could all call home together.

Nothing's impossible for the good Lord, child. I hear Mama's voice whisper to me from the past, and as I look up to this never-ending sky that rolls with the land past forever, I feel like that whisper has waited for just this moment . . . waiting for just the right time for me to open the gift. And maybe waiting for just the right people to see it opened.

And like this journal, I feel like this is only the beginning . . .

Thank You, Lord, for giving all of us this new chance, for making me think that maybe crow might not be so hard to swallow after all, if everything works out.

. . . Of course, I'm not planning on telling *Jack* that just yet.

August 31, 1869 . . .

I just told Jack he shouldn't plan on serving that bird up yet.

We reached the valley only a short time ago, halting the wagons at the rise that would lead us to our new home. As we stepped out, the beauty of the land before us near took our breath away . . . almost too pretty to put to words.

Everywhere we looked there was color—wildflowers blanketing the valley clear up to the slopes of the immense mountains in the Absaroka Range with a patchwork of lupine and fairy slipper and ones Lillie calls shooting stars. Three little cabins stood in the distance, barely visible in the heart of the valley, and I could see, just beyond them, a wide spring flowing, necklaced by cottonwoods. Our collies, Jasper and Honey, took off for the spring, barking. Then the cattle and horses saw it, too, taking off in a tired trot for the water. We all grinned at each other, then laughed as Rose quickly led the boys down the slope. So knee-deep was the grass it almost covered their heads. Patrick and John-Charles were stumbling like drunks on their little legs, trying to keep up, and suddenly Lillie, Jessie, and me were running, too, hitching up our skirts, laughing as we headed down the hill and came to a stop in front of the cabins that are to be our homes. And that's when I felt the poetry of the moment die inside of me.

Standing before us was three of the shabbiest log cabins I'd ever seen, the doors hanging sideways like loose teeth to show dirt floors inside. The roofs were dirt, too, with weeds and wildflowers springing every which way in an almost comical fashion—like a Sunday-go-to-meeting hat that had seen better times. The front yard of the main cabin was bare and . . . imagine . . . *dirt*, too, trampled down by horses and men too busy to worry for looks.

Jessie, Lillie, and I stepped through the door of the first cabin we came to and found . . . dirt. Jasper and Honey, who were belly-wet from the spring, came trotting in, looked up at me like it had to be a mistake, then went and lay down outside the door.

I admit, there was a part of me that wanted to give in and have a good cry.

I felt like I'd stepped back eight years in time and was standing in the shack of the little mining camp that was Quinn's and my first home, feeling the horror again. Then I thought of all the miles, of what we'd gave up, all of us living in cramped quarters for over two years in Virginia City, scrimping and scraping, for *this*. When I looked over at Lillie and saw the tumble of emotions crossing her pretty face, for some reason I thought of Mrs. Murphy standing next to me and the words she'd spoke that day in California.

"Don't look too close at first, honey," she'd said. *"Not till you're more settled. I remember coming to this very shack and thinking, I've come through dust, dirt, mud, and more dirt for this? If I'd had a gun, I think I would've shot my husband on the spot."* I heard myself telling the story, and as I did, I felt myself begin to smile, for I remembered the after of it, too, the way that little shack had become a home once I'd set my mind that it would.

Lillie looked down at the small swell of her belly, and I knew she was wondering what would come of her having a baby here, but then she smiled a kind of wry smile that caused a dimple to appear on her cheek.

"Well, I guess it's a good thing we don't have guns," she said, starting to chuckle, and Jessie and I did, too, in spite of it all.

"Lord, have mercy on the husbands of this group, is all I'm gonna say," Jessie said as she inspected the dull light shining through the slits in the logs. "'Cause they sure gonna need it."

It was along about then I noticed a darkening at the door, and we turned to see Stem standing with Rose. Stem took one look at our faces then turned to his constant shadow.

"Light quick t' yer wagon, sis, and git yer ma's Good Book," he told Rose. "We'll hold it in front of us. It'll be the only way t' turn the tide, I'm thinkin'." Rose grinned and took off in a dead run, relishing being a part of Stem's mission.

"He's a sharp one to smell trouble brewin' now, ain't he?" Jessie said, wrapping her arms across her chest to give him a stern look.

"It's a potent brew, Jess," Stem said amiably—but he kept his distance from us just the same.

"Ye call this our promiseland?" Jessie said, waving her arm around the room. Stem winced.

"Well, if ye squint yer eyes jes right . . . ," he started, and Jessie said, "Hmm," as he backed on out the door. I watched her look around, and I knew what she was thinking, because I was thinking it, too. We'd spent everything we had to get here, so there was nothing else to do but dig in and make it different. Jessie turned to us and pushed up the sleeves of her dress then, like she had almost read my mind. "Some fern and mud ought to do the trick on them cracks, don't ye think?"

It was only moments until we had started coming up with a plan on how to spruce up the cabins—but it was at least an hour before the men showed their faces again, bunches of wildflowers stretched out in each of their hands as a peace offering.

"It was my idea," Rose announced from somewhere behind Stem, and the men looked so sheepish we all couldn't help but laugh.

After the laughter died down, we decided on cabins. Quinn and I are to take the center cabin, being that it has a loft we can make over for Rose and Patrick's room. Jack and Lillie will have the cabin on the right, closer to the spring, and Stem and Jessie will take the one to the left of us. Coy's taking over the bunkhouse, being our "bachelor" of the bunch.

So *much* work to be done . . . I best get to it if we have any hopes of sleeping "indoors" by nightfall. Rose, who wants to be *outdoors* with the men, is grumbling under her breath as I quickly pen this, saying she never heard of sweeping a floor that was dirt anyhow.

Later—Such a good night in spite of our rough start.

Lillie, Jessie, and I were getting dinner set out on the makeshift table we'd set up in front of the main cabin just as evening was coming on us when I saw Lillie smile softly, looking up from time to time as she worked. Finally I stopped what I was doing and followed her gaze to the distance. The sun was just beginning to set, lighting up the tops of the mountains with a ridge of goldlike fire, and I was awed seeing it happen like that right before my eyes. Like seeing God put the finish to a great painting.

"This view makes up for a lot, doesn't it?" Lillie said then, and I nodded. "It reminds me of Jack," she added, and Jessie and me must've looked shocked for she laughed softly.

"When I first saw your brother, Callie, right off I thought, *Oh, he's too good-looking to trust,*" Lillie explained. "Then I fell in love with him and his charm shortly after that."

We chuckled, and Lillie smiled, turning back to the mountains. "Odd thing is, I have the same feeling about this land . . ."

I think we all feel that way, like we've started to fall in love with the land in spite of the work before us. As we sat around the dinner table tonight, speckled with lanterns, I could hear it in all the voices. "Look at those mountains, will you?" one would say. "How 'bout that spring—I ain't ever tasted water so cold in summer," another would say, and I realized it wasn't a flashy kind of love but a hopeful one, the kind that wished for more than just a night to rest their heads, but for a lifetime . . . a place to finally call home.

It was then I felt right to open and read from our family Bible, and I was surprised when the book opened to a page with a tiny faded flower tucked in the crease. "Rooster fights," Mama called them, with their purple edges and little yellow faces. I looked at the scripture my mama must have underlined years ago: "They that sow in tears shall reap in joy," it said.

As I read the scripture out loud, I felt a lump in my throat, remembering Mama. I saw the unshed tears shining in Jack's eyes, too, saw him looking down as he worried the brim of his hat. Jack, even in his wildest, reckless days, would turn to butter over Mama. "Sow in tears . . . ," he said, not looking up, and Rose picked that time to pipe in.

"Mama," she said, looking thoughtful. "If Jesus helped Grandma Wade reap joy, He'll help us, too. He's not suspicious. Pa said He's not a *suspector* of persons." There was such an earnestness to her face we all grinned and nodded—trying our best not to laugh—and I asked Stem to lead us in saying grace. He looked at me in surprise—then to Jessie who was fairly beaming at him.

"Age before beauty, isn't that what ye like to say, old man?" Coy said, grinning.

"If'n yer beauty, we're all in trouble," Stem countered, and we all laughed, joining hands around the table. I felt we were joined together at that moment by more than hands—but hearts, too. And as Stem began, his dry old voice humbled in thanks, I had the oddest feeling, as if Jesus Himself had sat down at that dingy, makeshift table, smiling as He joined hands with our weary but happy little group of travelers.

September 1, 1869 . . .

I felt like rubbing my eyes this morning to check if I were dreaming or not when I woke to find myself lying on the bedding I'd laid out across the fresh-swept dirt floor last night. Jasper and Honey crept over and peered down at me as if to see whether I'd come to my senses yet, and I couldn't help but smile. Like everyone else we love, the two pups had drifted into our lives one day, taken pity on us, and decided to stay. Now Jasper looked like he was wondering if the decision had been a good one, but Honey's great brown eyes were filled with compassion. I got up and let them out and stood watching them for a moment as they bounded through the tall grass. The sun was already burning a hole through the night sky, peeking fingers of light through the slits in the mountains, and I watched as only moments later the valley came to life, splashed with vivid blues, greens, and yellows, and I felt my heart lift at the beauty of it. Jasper and Honey barked merrily, forgetting the little cowards they'd been last night, begging and scratching at the door until Quinn let them in, only to become fierce guards, growling once they were inside the door.

I can't blame them too much. Sitting out here, even I can't help but think how everything looks better with the sun shining . . .

I best close for now. The natives will soon be stirring, and I haven't yet got the coffee made.

We have all worked so hard today, the men pounding, pounding, pounding with their hammers, trying to make our little cabins livable. Jessie, Lillie, and me set to unpacking our wagons and cleaning everything in sight. Quinn made us some shelves and a little counter for our "kitchen" from our packing boxes, and I filled the logs with "chinking" Jessie made up for each of us, then stretched and tacked burlap over the dirt floor before laying our rugs down. We brought the beds in next, Rose and Patrick's going to the loft, Quinn's and mine in the little curtained-off room. Then I dressed them fine with quilts. Next was Mama's old rocker. I sat it by the fireplace with another rag rug I'd made put at its feet.

Then Quinn brought our cookstove in, and I no sooner had a little fire stoked in it to start dinner when Patrick brought me in a baby squirrel. "A friend for Homey," as he calls Honey. Rose looked up at me so innocent with those pale blue eyes like her pa's, red hair all askew, declaring solemnly she had had nothing to do with it. John-Charles's eyes danced with laughter, reminding me so much of Jack, but he remained quiet as a church mouse, too, as if weighing his odds, his coppery face turning to study us all intently. "Just fell right into his lap," Rose added, then had the good sense to look injured as I shooed them all out.

"If you'd puckered your lip like I told you, she might've let us keep it," I heard her say to Patrick.

Stem, who had happened past our cabin just then, shook his head at me and grinned. "She's somethin' else, ain't she, Callie?" he said, shaking his head in wonder. There was something in the way he watched after Rose, cocking his old white head to one side with a thoughtful look, that touched my heart. Rose has had him wrapped around her little finger since she took her first breath—something they both knew but enjoyed knowing, too.

I tried not to smile, warning him about egging her on, but he just chuckled. "Yes ma'am," he said. Then, with a glint to his eyes, he added, "But there *ain't* no telling what she might do."

Later—I woke with a start this evening in my rocker, feeling something cold and clammy sliding over my face. As my eyes flew open, I saw three very impatient sets of eyes staring back at me.

It appears I had drifted off right in the middle of Daniel

being sent to the lions' den. Rose had decided slopping a wet rag across my face might do the trick to wake me.

"Sorry, Mama," she said, solemn as a judge, "but we just *couldn't* go to bed without knowing the end." She sat back down at my feet. Patrick hooked a dirty bare foot over his knee, clapping as I started to read again, and John-Charles, always the stoic little Indian, crossed his short legs, too, and listened intently.

Stem was right. There isn't any telling what Rose might do.

September 2, 1869 . . .

My arms are so sore. Sent Rose to milk the cow this morning while Patrick went for kindling for me. I got the "kitchen" cleared only to turn around and set to baking four loaves of bread—hope it will be enough for our crew. Lillie is making a stew, and Jessie is taking care of dessert. We've decided we like dining "out" and will keep it up as long as the weather holds. The cabins are a bit warm for dining in. It got so warm in the kitchen I came out here to write this. Beautiful scenery—the valley, the mountains, and the sky . . . so much sky. I don't think I'll ever get tired of looking.

Quinn just came trotting by with the pretty filly Rose calls Midnight, saying how I looked like a pretty girl with my red hair "like that." I put a hand to my head and was startled to find in my rush this morning that I'd forgot to pull my hair up.

I told Lillie and Jessie as we struck out to pick berries, if I wasn't careful, I'd end up looking as wild as this land.

They looked at each other then back to me, and we couldn't help but laugh. We *all* looked pretty "wild" compared to when we first got here, our "primping" going by the wayside with all the work. But our laughter seemed to say it wasn't such a bad "trade" to finally have a place to call home again.

"Besides," Lillie said, "wild can be pretty, too."

"If ye squint yer eyes jes right," Jessie said wryly.

September 3, 1869 . . .

More work today. I kept Rose indoors with me to help finish unpacking the rest of our things—which was work itself as she proceeded to tell me how being inside "purely takes all the fun out of living." It wasn't until she came across the little box that held all of my journals and asked if she could look at them that I sensed a change in her.

"It's like you still have all those people here with you," Rose said softly as she gingerly turned the pages of one of my journals. "Is that why you like keepin' a journal, Mama?" she asked, and I admit, her words took me back for a moment as I sat down on my bed next to her, looking at the soft honey-red hair that fell across her face as she studied the pages. I have always told Quinn that Rose is an odd mixture of us all: one minute daring as she takes off on one of the horses bareback, the next comical, the next thoughtful and so soft-hearted . . .

"This one's the day I was born," she said, smiling as she looked up at me.

"One of the best days of my life," I said, hugging her to me. Rose, being Rose, squirmed after a bit and asked to go help with the horses. As I watched her run out the door, I found myself drawn again to the box of journals, too. There, lying on top, was the first journal I'd ever wrote in, telling of our journey from Missouri to California. As I opened to the beginning, I found myself thinking how odd it was seeing all of our lives changing with just the turn of a page . . . Turn a page back, and my sister Rose is still alive, another few pages and Pa is there, too. I couldn't help thinking it would be something if life could really be fixed that easy.

I told Quinn about my thoughts when we had the chance to take a walk together after dinner, following the little trail past the new half-built corral to the spring.

Quinn dipped the pail in the water then looked off toward the sun setting behind the mountains in the distance. "'Twould be something, lass," he said softly, then he looked down at me with a look we had shared through our years of marriage. A look that spoke of memories, of loss and endurance and love . . . Then he cocked his head to one side, thoughtful, and I knew he was listening to the sounds of our family talking around the little bonfire Jack had made after dinner. We heard Coy and Stem bantering, then the children all laughed at something, and I saw Quinn smile softlike.

"But then, wouldn't we be missin' out on what's to come if we were always to turn back?" he said, taking my hand as we walked back up the trail. I smiled up at him, feeling such love in my heart.

"I think God must shake His head a lot over my wonderings," I admitted then, and Quinn chuckled.

"'Tis my belief the good Lord favors honest hearts, lass,

over the false ones. Perfect is in heaven. It's the tryin' that counts, I'm thinkin' . . ."

I looked at Quinn, really looked at him, and I thought of all we'd been through together, of how his words to me, entwined with our faith, always seem to make life better . . .

"Do you ever wonder what's next?" I asked him then, hooking my arm in his as he grinned down at me.

"With a family like ours?" he said, opening the door of our cabin for me. "All the time, lass, all the time."

Now, as I sit writing this, I can't help but wonder what's next, too. But I must leave my wondering for another day. I am *so* tired . . .

But it is a good tired.

September 4, 1869 . . .

Quinn and I both came down with a stomachache this evening. Coy, who was voted "doctor," came in, tipped his hat back, and announced we had "huckleberry overdose," a wide grin spreading across his dark face. But he did make us a drink of mint jelly diluted in cold water to settle our stomachs. The rest of the group came and went. We should've been embarrassed, but it seemed to take too much effort. We were so tired besides, from working all day, that all we could do was groan, lying next to each other in our curtained-off little room or dashing off to the bushes while Rose looked after Patrick.

After everyone left we were silent for a bit, then Quinn groaned again as he turned over to face me. I turned, too, and it seemed like we met each other with the exact expressions of misery on our faces at the same time. Quinn grinned in spite of his suffering and said, "I fear the honeymoon may be over."

"Already?" I said, and we both laughed in spite of ourselves.

Later—I'm feeling a bit better, although Quinn is still sleeping on and off. Rose and Patrick were having a time earlier, running and playing with Jasper and Honey, when I called out and asked Rose how her sampler was coming. There was a silence, then she said, "Fine, Mama," in the tone of a prisoner going to the gallows. I heard her drag her feet in a slow shuffle to the loft to fetch her sampler. I heard Patrick say then, loftily, "I'm glad I ain't a girl."

"I guess you won't mind fetching the wood, then, will you?" I said and heard silence for the second time, then, "No ma'am," as the door opened and shut and Patrick headed outside.

Sometimes it's hard to be a parent—especially when you want to laugh.

September 5, 1869 . . .

Quinn and I are feeling much better.

Warm, pretty day—not too many left like it, Jack says—which is why we all agreed to ride out for a tour of the countryside. Rose, Patrick, and John-Charles hooted with joy when they found out, as they were prepared to endure the Sabbath indoors. I admit I was feeling a bit guilty when we first headed out so quick after prayer. But as our horses began to work their way slowly through the valley, past our cattle getting fat on the wild hay in the meadows, up toward our "guards of the valley," the mountains, I began to feel God's presence all around us in all the unexpected beauty and grandeur. Everything looked so clean and pure—the view was like nothing I've ever witnessed. . . . "*On the seventh day He rested*" came to me, and I thought if ever there were a spot on earth *He* would choose to rest on, this would be it.

Jack must have sensed what I was feeling because he looked over his shoulder at me and grinned then, pulling his horse back to wait for me.

"Ain't no better church than this, is there, sis?" he said with that big, easy grin of his as he sidled up next to me. I told him I couldn't imagine one, and I felt my heart swell as I looked into my brother's green eyes. The haunting, the always searching look that had been there since we were kids, had been eased since, as Jack liked to say, he'd made his peace with God . . . , and I couldn't help wishing our mama had lived long enough to see that.

I stayed back as Jack finally rode off to catch up with the rest of them and just watched as they trailed on, Stem and Jessie in the lead, so deep in gazing at the mountains that Jessie forgot to be scared on her horse . . . Lillie and Jack grinning at each other like kids, then turning to look upward, too . . . Coy cocking his head to one side as he gazed at an eagle soaring down over the valley, and Rose pulling back on Midnight and watching the eagle, too. Then I saw Quinn catch up to John-Charles and Patrick on their ponies, pointing something out to them in the distance. Quinn looked back at me once and smiled and waved, and in his smile, I saw he was as struck by the beauty of it all as I was.

As we all were. It was as if we'd found our sermon in God's creation, speaking to us through the mountains, the trees, and sky . . .

"Is this our promiseland?" I whispered, so full of hope, sitting on my horse in the stillness, but all I heard was the echo of my own voice asking *me*.

I wonder what my answer will be . . .

September 6, 1869 . . .

Sunny today—but a bit cooler. I was hanging wash out when I was caught by the sight of Jack and Coy down at the corrals, breaking a horse. There was something about the sight of Jack on that horse with the morning sun glowing orange behind them that drew me to watch; I saw the horse rear up again as I came to stand next to Coy, its eyes looking wild as it tried to buck Jack from its back. But Jack hung on—not by just strength, it seemed—but by sensing what the horse felt.

After what seemed an eternity, the horse finally gave in to Jack, and I saw him motion to Coy to let them out of the corral. We watched as Jack took off across the valley in a full run, and Coy looked over at me and smiled, soft. "That brother of your'n is *good*," he told me. "I ain't quite figured out how he does it, but it's like they trust his ways."

As I watched Jack push the horse faster I couldn't help thinking how they both seemed to be enjoying it, and it hit me what it was that horse sensed in Jack. My brother, who had loved and lost and learned to love again, understood more than most that sometimes you have to give up your freedom to get it.

Quinn came in from cutting hay tonight to tell us that we will be going to town first thing in the morning for supplies. How strange that sounds—*town*. Even Virginia City seems less than a memory now and more like something I might have made up.

It will be interesting to find out what this place has to offer . . .

September 7, 1869 . . .

They say the test of good manners is to be patient with bad ones . . . I admit I've failed the test today. *I truly want to be good, Lord. But sometimes it's just plain hard.*

Our trip to "town" took us through some of the roughest yet wildly beautiful countryside, through the valley, then up once more along narrow passes that wound around the mountains like a disjointed snake. I kept craning my neck to spot anything that might pass as a town and found nothing but wilderness until an hour or so later. Then it appeared quick, as if it had sprung up from the dirt before our very eyes. There was a big sign as we entered town, all flourishes and curlicues, telling us we'd come to "Audrey," but it almost seemed a joke as I looked around. There was a blacksmith, a few crude log huts, and then, on the other side of the thoroughfare, a mercantile that seemed to be the best-looking building of the bunch.

Patrick asked, "Is this the *United of States*, Mama?" which brought a good round of laughter from us all.

Then it was: "There's the hens, girls," Stem declared, grinning, "best get to peckin'." The other men chuckled as we turned to see three women standing in front of the mercantile like they were expecting us. The one in the middle was fair, but angry-looking. She appeared to lead the little group, for she turned and said something to the other ladies, who quickly took their leave, then she went back in the mercantile and I saw her go and stand behind the counter and wait.

Rose took my hand as we headed for the store, pale blue eyes so much like her pa's staring up at me. "She looks like Mother Long," she whispered, breathless, and I almost asked, "Who?" but we were already at the mercantile.

I couldn't help looking about in shock at how much they had for such a small town: on the floor, barrels of flour, white and middling; next to that, a barrel of molasses and another of vinegar and one of salt pork. Hams, shoulders, and breakfast bacon hung from the rafters. Toward the back there were pickle jars and milk crocks, and beyond that the farm tools. The side of the counter where the woman stood had big glass jars of striped candy that Rose eyed with longing, and behind her on the shelf were crocks of honey, coffee, and tea.

Mrs. Audrey, as she introduced herself, appeared young at a closer look. I say *appeared* because, though her blonde hair was fine-looking and there didn't seem to be a single line under the dark eyes that pierced us, there was something *old* about her, something almost bitter. A smallish man stood behind the counter, too, a ways down, filling egg baskets—three dozen for a quarter—and looked as out of place as a chicken in a wolf's den. Two young girls ran in, grabbed up some candy, and almost dashed back out before they could be introduced. Zora and Nora, the Audreys' twins, nodded to us, gave Rose the once-over with a kind of disdain, then left before you could blink. I went to say something to Rose, who was looking so crestfallen, but Mrs. Audrey was already there, leaning over the counter toward me with a look of alarm.

"Really, Mrs. McGregor," she said. "Puh-haps next time y'all should leave yo-ah *pee*-ple home." Rose and I turned to follow Mrs. Audrey's gaze, and we saw Jessie pointing out some goods to Lillie. I felt the blood go to my cheeks like it did when I got mad.

"We . . . well, we don't really allow . . . ," she lowered her voice, dipping her head toward mine, "*negras* in ah sto-ah," she drawled out, and before I could say a thing I heard a rustling from behind one of the shelves.

"Casting stones again, Leah?" a woman's voice called out. "I would have thought you had your hands full with me."

The woman appeared from the other side of the shelves then, slim and lovely, very refined, and not bothering to look our way as she set her few items down, took her gloves off, and laid money down for her purchases. She looked right at Mr. Audrey.

"You have so many customers you can afford to turn them away now?"

"No ma'am, Miss Cain," Mr. Audrey said, and I was surprised to see him smile until Mrs. Audrey huffed loudly. Then he dropped his eyes a bit.

"Well, Percy, I'm finished here. I believe you can tally

this up," Miss Cain said then, and the way she said it made you think she wasn't sure he could do much else. Mr. Audrey's bald head flushed red under the few sparse hairs that were combed sideways, but he totaled her up and she was out the door before you could blink.

Lillie and Jessie joined me and Rose near the front, and we turned to watch the woman walk away from the mercantile with a kind of easy manner and light smile on her face—like she had a good joke but hadn't found the right person to share it with. I happened to glance back then, and I saw Mrs. Audrey was watching the woman, too, with a grim look on her face. I couldn't help but ask who she was.

"Ringleader of Sin," was all Mrs. Audrey provided, her face creased in distaste.

Jessie appeared to be enjoying her discomfort, but as I glanced at Lillie, I saw the frown on her forehead and the bolt of cloth she was holding hanging limp in her hands, and I knew she was thinking of her own past—and future as far as the *good women* of the town were concerned, and I felt my temper get the best of me.

"Ringleader, huh? Well, maybe next time you can introduce us, then," I said casually and saw Mrs. Audrey's face go sour on me. I grabbed Rose's hand, and she grinned up at me, then we all marched out of the mercantile without buying a thing on our lists. I know it's not right, but I confess wild horses couldn't have got me back in there as mad as I was.

Not long after that the men came back, and we told them what had happened. And Jack, being *Jack*, decided to go fetch the supplies himself, striding with purpose with his buckskins and hair long as an Indian's into the mercantile.

"You can forget the castor oil if you want to, Uncle Jack," Patrick hollered as he leaned over the back of the wagon, and John-Charles laughed. I don't know what happened, but he came out with that grin of his, supplies stacked up near past his head, and we all pulled out shortly after that, having had our fill of town.

It wasn't until I turned to look back that I saw the pretty dark-haired woman again. She was walking toward the blacksmith's, and I saw a young Indian woman sitting by the side of the dust-choked road, rocking a good-sized bundle in her arms. Neither of the women looked at each other, but as Miss Cain passed I noticed the cans of milk that fell from her bag—noticed, too, the Indian woman snatch them up quick and hide them in her blanket without missing a beat . . .

"Ringleader of Sin," I said under my breath, and I heard Jessie chuckle from the back of the wagon.

"She *would* be worth meeting, don't you think?" she said then, and Lillie burst out laughing. "You two beat all," she said.

"What's so funny, Mama?" Rose asked, always wanting to be in the know. I smiled at her. "Just a little family joke is all," I said, and when Lillie turned and smiled at me, I saw the unshed tears in her eyes. Saw the hope, too.

"That's what God put families together for, Callie, to believe in each other when we can't believe in ourselves . . ." Mama's voice whispers to me tonight as I write this. And the truth of it was in Lillie's eyes when I asked her to be the one to read from the family Bible tonight after

dinner. How gingerly she opened that Bible, her voice soft but filled with emotion as she read each line of scripture with such care and gratefulness . . .

Lillie was still reading when the men went down to check on the cattle, her lips moving with the words as she rocked John-Charles in her arms. Seeing her like that, I couldn't help remembering the time she told me how she had gotten hold of our family Bible by accident, of how she had been so heartbroke when Jack had to leave Virginia City because of those outlaws. Then Coy's pa, Duel, had rode out to go help Jack. The next thing she knew, she had a letter in her hands from Jack, telling her Duel had been killed and asking her to see he was buried proper. The Bible had come back with Duel's body, so at first she thought it was his. Then one night when she was low, she opened it and saw our family page and knew it was Jack's Bible.

"I thought to myself only good families keep things like that," she'd told me. "So I was sure I wouldn't fit in—that you all couldn't love someone like me . . . But you know what I learned? I learned that because you come from a family that loved, that's why you could love me." I still remember her hopeful smile then. "So maybe one day John-Charles and my new little one will be able to say they had a good ma and pa. That they were loved . . ."

Lillie looked up once as we started clearing the dishes and made to rise, but I told her to go on reading.

It was Jessie that put to words what I was thinking as we walked to the spring together to get the water. "Never saw someone so grateful," she said, dipping her pail into the stream. "Makes a person ashamed to ask for anything more than what we've got."

"We have a lot, don't we, Jessie?" I said, and she cocked her head to one side and looked at me for a moment, thoughtful.

"Yes, I guess we do at that," she said finally and smiled.

The pretty Indian woman begging outside the black-smith's today is the smith's *wife*. Stem says the young man is a pure whiskey soak if ever there was one, that "Mr. Carey" had only looked up once from the horseshoe he was tapping on, eyes all red and bleary, to ask Quinn and Jack if we had any horses to sell. Stem said he had ignored Stem completely—and his own wife, too, when she'd come in pleading with him over something.

Bless Miss Cain for giving the poor woman those cans of milk.

Later—Well, I have found out who "Mother Long" is. I overheard Rose telling Patrick a story tonight, whispering of "the perfect murderess" who became known as the "banditti of the plains." Rose must've thought over the "plains" part, because then I heard her add breathlessly, "Chubs, I think she's come to hide in these here moun-tains . . . to become the banditti of the *mountains*."

I have no doubt it was Jack that smuggled her another one of those awful dime novels.

It wasn't much later that I was woke by a stout little shadow leaning over me. "Mama? Are you awake?" Patrick whispered loud enough to wake the dead. "I come to check on you and Pa." He promptly climbed into the bed between us and whispered to me the whole sordid story, how Rose just *knows* Mrs. Audrey is really Mother Long. Even in the dim light, I could see his eyes were huge.

"Who's this Mother Long, then?" Quinn mumbled, turning over.

"The *bandanna* of the plains," Patrick whispered loudly again, and it was all I could do not to laugh as Quinn said, "The *what?*"

I'm awake now, and my two Irishmen, splayed out across the bed, have fallen sound asleep before they could hash out the whole story . . .

September 10, 1869 . . .

Lillie and I met the infamous "Ringleader of Sin" today.

It was shortly after breakfast when I heard the men talking amongst themselves about some of the cattle being missing as they hammered away, putting finishing touches to the new corral. Thinking it would give us a chance to see some of the countryside, I volunteered Lillie and me to go look for them. Jessie was quick to offer to watch our babes, so it was settled. They all grinned like it was a fine joke, then Quinn said, "Do ya think ya two can hannel the cattle alone then, lass?" and I said, "I did in California, didn't I?"

Then Jack says to Lillie, "What about wolves?" and she gave Jack a wry look before mounting up next to me.

"I worked in a saloon," she said, "so I guess I might know a thing or two about wolves." Lillie winked at me, and we both grinned at each other.

"I guess you see why I had to marry her," Jack sighed, and Quinn shook his head.

"Would've thought Callie to be enough for one family," he said, and I gave him a look and told him we would have the cattle back before dinner. As Lillie and I rode off, we could hear their laughter follow us clear past the spring and up the slope. Once we were out of sight, I turned to Lillie and asked her if she had a clue how to handle cattle.

"Well, I guess we'll figure it out once we find them," she said, looking at me with more confidence than I think she truly felt, and we both laughed. But it wasn't too long after that, we lost our sense of humor.

We found the stray cattle, but they didn't seem the least bit interested in seeing us. I reined my mount to the right and told Lillie to go left, and just when we thought we had them, two of the culprits went right between us, trotting off a short distance away and soon chomping on grass again. This went on so that I started wondering if the cattle were making a game of us. It was growing hotter and hotter, and Lillie and I were fit to be tied. The cattle had scattered everywhere, and our faces were smudged with dirt and sweat when we suddenly noticed we had an audience. We both turned at the same time to see Miss Cain, dressed as fine as the day we saw her in the mercantile, all embroidery and lace. Her hat—just as fine—was tossed to one side in the grass, and I saw her hair was darker than I remembered, dark and shiny like a raven's wing. She looked so pretty it still doesn't seem possible—because she was sitting astride a fallen log, corncob pipe clenched between her lips!

"Ladies, I was born and bred in Boston—intellectual

hub of the universe by most accounts," she speculated, tapping the pipe against her boot. "But this isn't Boston, so I'll give it to you plain. Best thing you can do is yell at them. They're dumb creatures—a bit like our two-legged counterparts," she said, winking. "Which is why I raise hogs now." She grinned at us then, hopping off her perch, and Lillie and I couldn't help laughing outright. She briskly introduced herself to us as "Willa," and shook our hands. Then she looked close at Lillie, squinting her eyes. "You look to be expecting," she announced, then didn't wait for a reply before she went on. "There is a doctor in these parts—or at least he says he is—he spends most of his time looking for gold. He isn't much of a miner, either, though, if that speaks for his character. But at the least, you know he's around if you think you might need him." She nodded to us and sauntered off toward her own horse, and within moments she was gone.

"Was she really here, or did I just imagine all of that?" Lillie said, turning to look at me. I shook my head in wonder.

"I'm a pretty big imaginer," I told her, "but I don't think even I could've come up with all of that."

Now, writing this, I *know* I couldn't have.

There *was* something about her, though, that seemed to inspire us. Without any more talk, Lillie and I turned back to the cattle, hawing and whistling at them like two old cowpokes, and rounded up the surprised mama and yearling in short time, leading them and the rest of the wayward little group home, tails tucked between their legs like kids caught playing hooky.

The men are impressed by us as well. I notice, too, that

Lillie, who was so unsure of herself hours earlier, even has a bit of a swagger in her step as she walks by.

Later—I've been thinking a lot about Willa Cain this evening for some reason.

I feel almost like she flung that greeting out to us then retreated quick before we had a chance to say anything back. Like maybe she was afraid of what she might get in return. Lillie and Jessie think it's because of the women in town. "I've dealt with their kind before," Lillie said slowly. "It's a wonder she talked to us at all."

"Loneliness will tromp right over fear if the loneliness is strong enough," Jessie said. "Being out here all by yourself, that's got to be some kind of lonely."

Some kind of lonely . . . It's hard to imagine what would keep a Boston-bred lady out here, rising early day in and day out to feed stock and lug water, planting one foot after another all day long then heading back home to bed with no one to tell your worries, your fears, to . . .

I have to wonder how she does it. Does she turn her face up to the night sky and have her talks with You like I do, Lord? Or is she really alone? I hope not, but I can't help but wonder . . .

September 15, 1869 . . .

Sunny today, but windier than usual. Fall is coming. It's in the wind, in the grass that's already turning a honey color, and in our pace to get things done before winter sets in for good.

I've already carried two buckets of water from the spring, and I expect I'll have to make another run before all is said and done today. I noticed, though, my arms aren't nearly as sore as they were. Maybe I'm getting stronger.

September 18, 1869 . . .

We have all worked so hard today, pitching in to help the men dig a rough dirt dam to trap water from the spring for another watering hole. I'd just sat down to write this when Jessie came to tell me that Stem "'fessed up" that he had glimpsed Willa Cain's place while out looking for a stray. He said she had a small but pretty frame house, a milk cow, some chickens, and *the cleanest hogs you've ever laid eyes on.*

"He said she was high-stocked with brains, too—though he sounded suspicious of that part," Jessie said, grinning.

"A lot of detail for someone just trotting by," I said wryly, and Jessie chuckled.

"Ye'd never imagine it by looking at him," she said, shaking her head, "but that old man's got women beat for bein' in the know of things." We both laughed and looked toward the corral where Rose was following close on Stem's heels.

"Them two is a *pair*, ain't they?" Jessie said then, and I was surprised to see her eyes mist over a bit. "Just like family," she said, almost to herself, and I wondered if Jessie was thinking of the family she'd lost before the war.

"We *are* family," I said, smiling. "Jack says who else but us knows everything about each other—and loves each other anyway?"

"Jack say that?" she grinned, surprised, and I nodded, linking my arm in hers as we walked back to the cabin together to start dinner.

"And if *Jack* says it, you know it must be true," I said, and we both laughed.

Later—An old miner showed up at the ranch just in time for dinner this evening and to pass some news along as well.

It appears he and some partners are panning gold a short distance away. He saw the smoke and said he "thought to investergate." As it's custom in the "territory" to offer food and lodging to strangers that happen by, we invited him to stay. Over dinner he told us he had come west before the "wah" to hunt and trap. He made it well known to all of us that he'd been first to arrive in these parts and had "witnessed it as it all began." The question of Adam and Eve came to mind, but I bit my tongue, smiling to myself as he then declared himself as "the one who pioneered the territory." While his accent leaves no doubt of his southern heritage, he and Stem were soon thick as thieves, talking about old times.

"This dern place is on the verge of gettin' crowded," Stem said at one point, spitting tobacco, to which the old-timer tore off a great piece of his own tobacco and chewed energetically, nodding and spitting in agreement.

"Civilization is comin'," he declared somberly, and I picked that point to speak up and ask about the doctor Willa Cain had mentioned for Lillie. The old fellow nodded his head and told us there was a doctor-turned-miner in "these here parts." Wrinkling his crusty brow, he said, "I ain't sure how good he is with actual doctorin'. But he's a mite good tooth puller." He smiled big enough for us to see the "Doc's" handiwork.

He had no teeth.

Stem did tell us all later that our visitor had confessed on his way out that a traveling preacher is in town to hold a "tent meetin' on the morrow." He shook his head as the women of the group exclaimed, as if to ask what the world was coming to, but I could tell he was pleased at being the bearer of such news.

It's been nearly a year since any of us have heard a real sermon. Lillie, Jessie, and I talked it over then made quick work of the dishes so we could try to find Willa Cain's place before it turns too dark.

More later—

We found Willa Cain's place easy enough—but she made it plain to us that she isn't interested at all in going to hear the new preacher. "I have never benefited from such things before, so, no, I don't believe I'm interested," she said in a voice that was so proper I wasn't sure it was the same woman.

None of us knew quite what to do after that. I told Lillie and Jessie that in spite of her acting the way she did, I thought I'd saw a kind of longing in her eyes, too.

I wasn't sure if it was true or just imagined it—until I glanced back as our wagon pulled away and saw a feeling on Willa's face I can't quite explain. Now that I write this,

I think I know what it was . . . the look of a dog that had been whipped so hard it would shy away from even a kind hand no matter how hungry it was . . . because it had been broke of hoping . . .

September 19, 1869 . . .

Such a blessing to finally be able to spend the Sabbath in a "church."

I admit I didn't know what to expect when we first came upon the tent the preacher had set up at the edge of town, surrounded by buckboards and bonnets as it was. The tent itself was huge—the oddest combination of skins and scraps of cloth I'd ever seen. There was a "barker," of sorts, standing outside the tent. "Th' rule is, Nothin' to be bought or sold hereabouts," he declared. "Just come an' hear the message."

The first thing that surprised me when we walked into the tent was the number of people who had gathered there. Good news travels fast—and far—by the looks of some of their trail-worn clothes. I saw Mrs. Audrey and her family—saw that Rose did, too, for she leaned over and whispered to Patrick and John-Charles, and I watched them stiffen and accept Rose's hand as she led them with a look of ultimate sacrifice to their seats. It wasn't until the rest of us got seated that I spotted the preacher who stood quietly reading his Bible at the front of the tent. He was quite large in size—six-foot-four or better—at least as big as Quinn, if not bigger. And he was handsome enough, with brown, wavy hair and a strong but kind face. His suit was modest but clean, maybe a bit worn, too. But when his eyes looked up I felt as if they carried the knowledge of the burdens of the world . . . and hoped somehow to ease them.

He cleared his throat, then without much ado, he began to speak to all of us in a deep but gentle voice that drew us in. Rose, Patrick, and John-Charles sat so still I had to keep checking to make sure they were there. They never took notice of me, so spellbound they were with the preacher.

I will try to put the sermon to paper just as he spoke it.

"I want all of those that traveled the California and Oregon Trails to stand and be counted," he announced, and nearly everyone in the tent stood, chuckling, looking at each other. Then he told us to sit again.

"Long journey, wasn't it?" the preacher said, followed by "amens" all around. "Suffering along the way?"

Yes. Lord, yes.

"Sometimes you didn't think you could take another step. Sometimes you thought maybe God didn't hear you anymore—that maybe He was just too big and you were just too small."

There was tears in most of our eyes, quiet nods of heads, and the preacher smiled a comforting smile that seemed to be for each one of us personally.

"But just when you thought you were at your end, you came up over that hill, into that land . . . that town . . . that tent, and you found you had made it, you *had made it through* in spite of what you thought."

There was a good amount of silence as everyone fell deep in thought and memory. The preacher smiled again.

"It's the *journey* that I've come to talk to you about," he said. "The journey of our lives." He stepped forward then with a look of eagerness on his face, and Quinn looked over at me and smiled. "Don't you see? We're just travelers here, just passing through. Every day is another journey, but He's there to lead us through it—if we'll let Him, if we'll listen." He held up a worn Bible in his hands for all to see, and I noticed how huge his hands were, and how callused, too, like he had worked at more than studying with those hands. "This book is our map, folks. The direction to get us home—to our *real* home, that is. And that home is called heaven . . ."

"What be yer name, young feller?" an old-timer called from the silence of the crowd, and the preacher dipped his head a bit. "Well, you can just call me Preacher, if you need to call me anything. Only name I hope for you to remember is Jesus'."

He spoke of other things, too. Of loving our neighbors as Jesus loved us. And he asked us to remember that it was the *broken* ones Jesus went to—not the "fixed."

He said most folks in the Bible that God used were broken, and that was exactly why God used them, because they understood what it meant to be broken—and knew how good it felt to be fixed.

The last thing he said was for us to remember Jesus had been broken, too. That He had been slandered and left alone in His darkest hour, that He had been laughed at and beaten, put in prison and even killed. He said God made sure Jesus was raised back up so we could have Someone to talk to Who understood . . . Then Preacher said we should be the ones to follow that example—that we should *understand* for others, too.

"Hebrews says it best," Preacher said, looking up from

his well-worn Bible. "It says He can have compassion on those who are ignorant and going astray, since He Himself was also subject to weakness."

There was a whisper of a question then. "Aw, Harm, it jes means ya kin feel a feller's blisters better if ya've walked the road yerself," an old miner said to himself—apparently louder than he had planned, for the whole crowd overheard and tittered, but Preacher just smiled.

"I couldn't have said it better myself, brother," he said, earning some chuckles. Then he told us to bow our heads so we could close with a prayer.

Afterward, I couldn't help thinking as everyone started a slow trickle from the tent that there had been something about the preacher that seemed almost regal while he talked to us, like he was out of place in his own humble surroundings. When he greeted us after the service, I thought putting my hand in his was a bit like shaking paws with a noble lion.

I turned and looked just as he took Stem's hand, and suddenly it seemed like everything had went quiet around us. I saw Stem look up into the preacher's eyes.

"Ain't had much book learnin', but what ya said sounded right t' these ears, young feller," Stem said abruptly, then he looked down at his dark old hand, still resting in the preacher's. I saw him nod then, like he'd settled something with himself. "My mama was a godly woman," he went on. "She didn't have nothin' t' speak of, bein' a slave an' all. But I recall how her eyes would shine, talkin' of seein' Jesus a'fore she died. She used to say, 'I don' have nothin', so I don' worry 'bout nothin' for this earth. I jes keep my eyes fixed on the Lord.'" Stem cocked his head sideways and squinted up at the preacher. "Ya kindly remind me of her, Preacher."

"I count that as fine company to be in," Preacher said softly, and I could see he was touched more than I expected—more than any of us imagined. "By the way, what do folks call you?"

"I was born Justice," Stem supplied. "But my friends call me Stem."

"Justice?" the preacher said, and Stem stood a bit straighter in defense, used to folks finding it funny for an old black trapper to have such a name.

"My mama knew humor well enough, I guess," he said finally, and the preacher looked into Stem's eyes as a kind smile came to his face.

"Or maybe she knew her *son* well enough," he said.

Stem looked at the preacher one last time before we all walked away, and I felt like they had understood each other in some way I can't exactly explain.

I don't think Stem can explain it either. "Don't know why I gave sech a speech," he said under his breath as we headed for our wagons. "Ye'd think I'd drew enough attention in my youth t' last a lifetime." Jessie glanced over her shoulder and smiled—we both did, for we knew *Who* had led Stem to speak.

Oh, thank You, Lord, for this day, for touching our hearts in the way only You know how to do . . .

I was writing in this journal when we were surprised by a visit from Willa Cain. She seemed to want to know how our trip had went, but it was like she wasn't sure how to ask—or how to get an answer without appearing to care. I think Stem sensed her feelings, for I saw him watch her from the corner of his eye as he talked partly to Rose—but mostly to Willa.

"Well, sis, I'll allow I ain't never seen sech a man that 'pears so fierce but kin hold a babe so tender in that big paw of his'n. He ain't the judgin' type, neither," Stem said, punctuating the thought with a stream of tobacco. I saw Willa's face was wistful. Then, catching me looking, she pursed her lips and cocked an eyebrow.

"What's this fellow's name, then?" she said, trying to sound casual, like she wasn't that interested.

"He says to jes' call him Preacher, said the only name that was important was Jesus'," Stem said, shaking his old head and smiling. "Ain't ever heard a man talk like him, an' I've heard a lot of jaw work in my time, that's fer sure."

Willa sniffed.

"Well, he sounds shifty to me," she said, rising from the table. "Let's take a walk, shall we, Callie?" she said then, real properlike, and Stem caught my eye and winked.

We took our walk down by the spring, just Willa and me, talking about little nothings, really, until she stopped for a bit when we were caught by surprise as a fish suddenly jumped up from the water, and we laughed. I saw Willa glance down at a ring she wore on her finger. It was a fancy gold affair, I could see that much. And I saw that the stone was missing, too, and wondered if she'd had to sell the stone. Willa caught me looking and got a secret kind of look on her face then brushed her hands through her skirt as if to hide the ring. Then, for some reason I don't think either of us knew, she just started talking.

43

She told me she wasn't as crazy as most folks thought—that sometimes crazy was smart.

"One thing that wasn't smart was me getting married," she said. "Some gentleman would start talking to me, start wanting to court, and I would think, *Well, it's the proper thing to do.* But for me there wasn't anything proper about it—no matter how much folks frown on a woman being on her own. I was just trying to replace something I had lost, and you can't replace people . . ."

She fell silent for a bit and we just walked, but I kept quiet, having a feeling she wasn't finished—and she wasn't.

She went on and told me she'd not been divorced from her second husband a month when men just started "happening by" her ranch to look her over. "Like checking a brood mare," she said with a grin.

"I read somewhere if Indians thought you were crazy, they would leave you alone, so I thought to try it out. I would spot some fellow coming down my road in a wagon or on a horse, and I'd say to myself, 'Okay, what's it going to be today?' Then I would greet him in whatever language I chose." She grinned again. "I'm fluent in five, so it made for interesting conversation." We both chuckled, then Willa went on. "Some decided to use the excuse of breeding their boars with my sows," she said. "So I washed them up good—even knitted booties for them to wear—and informed the poor gent standing there that his boar was too dirty for my 'girls.' Folks in town started saying I was crazy, that all my sinful ways had caught up to me . . ." Willa turned and looked at me thoughtfully. "So I decided I didn't need their religion."

"I didn't mean to offend you last night, Callie," she added. "I've taken quite a liking to you and your family."

Willa suddenly looked almost embarrassed at all she had told me, and she stood, shaking her skirts off then smoothing them over before she looked up at me again. "Well, this has been practically a speech for me," she said, turning toward her wagon. "So I guess I'll head home now."

"Come visit us anytime," I said, calling after her. "Not everyone thinks the same, you know." She stopped in her tracks, and I saw her look over her shoulder before she started toward her wagon.

"Perhaps you're right about that," was all she said, then she stepped up into her wagon and hawed her team on without looking back.

I don't know the whys of it, but there is something about Willa Cain that I feel drawn to, a yearning inside to show her things can be different—to help her, like the preacher said, to *understand* that God *is* there . . .

My mama used to say that sometimes we're the only Bible some folks will ever have the chance to read . . . *So, Lord, I'm asking You to help me. Help me to be Your Book so good she can't put it down until she's done . . .*

October 1, 1869 . . .

Well, my mama also used to say rudeness was the weak man's imitation of strength, too . . . I can see now why it's been so hard for Willa Cain to trust anyone around these parts. There are some folks that are mean just for the spite of it, and the man who came to buy one of our yearlings today is proof of that.

The man showed up as we were herding some of the horses to our new corral for branding. I was riding with Jack and Stem, coming down the slope at the west of the property, when I saw a short but thick-built man waving at Quinn in the distance. I don't know any other way to explain it than he looked seedy to me, and for some reason, I got a bad feeling in my stomach and nudged my horse on toward the corrals. Quinn had seen him, too, and hawed his team to a trot to catch up to him.

Somehow the filly Quinn had tied to the back of his wagon either balked or got tripped up, for as the dust started to settle around them, I saw she was tangled up in the lead rope and was nearly being dragged behind the wagon. I nudged my horse into a run and caught up with them just in time. Quinn started untying the horse and checking her out. He told me to go ahead and find out what the man wanted, so I did just that.

Mr. Carey, as he introduced himself, had been watching the scene from the yard. He laughed harsh as I rode up.

"Shoulda let yer man drag her," he said, looking up at me with bleary red eyes. "Horses are a lot like women—it's only the hard lessons they remember. You're a pretty thing, ain't ya?" he added then and grinned.

I admit I was shocked first, then mad, but remained cool as I asked him his business. He told me he'd come to buy a horse. He said, with a wave of his thick arm, that the horse he had was played out. I glanced over to his mount and saw the mare was in pitiful shape.

As a matter of fact, she looked to be so poorly cared for that I almost asked him to leave her, but then Quinn came up and I wasn't sure what to say. I did try my best to get

Quinn's attention, to warn him not to sell the filly to the man, but he kept talking to the man, all but ignoring me.

So as not to cause a scene, I waited until they had finished their business and watched after Mr. Carey, trotting down the trail on his poor mare and leading the pretty two-year-old filly behind in a tight grip. As soon as he was out of sight, I turned and told Quinn what Mr. Carey had said, and he gave me a look of disbelief at first. Then I saw his handsome face turn grim and hard all at once. He said it was the last horse the man would ever buy from us. He said, "Been my experience a man who shows cruelty to an animal is sure to do the same to his own kind."

"I *tried* to tell you," I said again to make sure he understood. He pretended not to, talking about all he had to get done, but I heard him start to whistle as he headed back for the corral, and I knew he *had* understood. We've been married long enough for me to know when Quinn starts whistling, it's because he's worried.

I *am* aggravated with him. But I blame myself, too, and now I'm just wishing I had said something before that awful man led our horse away.

October 2, 1869 . . .

Rose churns tonight up and down with the dasher, saying, "Come, butter, come. Peter standing at the gate, waiting for a butter cake." But it sounds more like a growl than a song. She isn't too happy with her pa after finding out we sold Midnight out from under her. Even though we both told her awhile back the horse was too skittish for her, she feels wronged.

It's the first overcast day I can recall since we've come here. It suits my mood, though. I feel like I'm brewing as I write this, like those clouds hanging over the mountains, still troubled about selling our horse to that man.

Like Rose, I wish we *could* take it back—but for different reasons.

I'm sure Quinn thinks I'm blowing it all out of proportion, but every once in a while I feel like I've come up on a stranger living in my house . . . like he doesn't understand how I feel . . .

Later—Quinn just brought me a pretty bouquet of wild-flowers, then we talked long into the night. The "stranger" has retreated to the shadows again, and we're together again, just like old times.

He told me tonight he hated when the silence edged in between us, and I agreed, but I told him something I'd remembered Mama telling me, too: Disagreeing is normal; it's lying to someone—to yourself—that's what's bad.

October 4, 1869 . . .

I was still having a hard time shaking the gloom of Mr. Carey's visit when Patrick brought me some flowers in this afternoon—a pretty but crumpled little bouquet of half-dead wildflowers. I put them in a little can of water and told him I would tuck some in this page to save. Just then Rose came in, taking it all in at a glance.

"They look pretty dead to me, Chubs," Rose announced with nine-year-old authority as she stood in the doorway, hands perched on her hips. Patrick gave her a withering look then looked down at his gift that, to him, had been ruined by her words. I could see his mind searching, grasping for something, *anything* to say back to her.

"Shut the door, Rose," he said, agitated, "'tis bloody windy out there!"

I didn't know whether to laugh or scold him. He had done such a perfect imitation of his father that if it weren't for the voice, I might've wondered. Quinn, who had been stoking wood in the fireplace, coughed. Knowing that cough, I hurriedly tried to explain that "bloody" wasn't a nice thing for a boy to say, sending Patrick and Rose off quick to finish their outside chores.

No sooner than the door shut behind them, Quinn turned to me, shaking his head, and said with a grin, "Where *does* the lad come up with these things?" Then he saw my look and had the good sense to look sheepish before we both burst out laughing.

October 5, 1869 . . .

Beautiful day. Made breakfast, cleaned, baked three loaves of bread, and sent Rose and Patrick off to chores, then decided to ride out to help the men bring cattle down closer to the valley. Truth is, I was itching to see *fall* close up, and it didn't disappoint me. Everything seemed ablaze. The honey-colored meadows were like the flickering of the flame that gained heat farther up the slopes as I rode through the larch and aspens towering over me in a burst of orange and gold fire, and I felt awed by the beauty of it all. When I reached the men, I could tell they were a bit awed, too. They were all working in a kind of grateful silence, like they'd been given a chance at something so special they didn't want to mess it up.

Like being in love and wanting it to last forever . . .

I took a quick drink of water from my canteen and handed it to Quinn, and we smiled at each other, our eyes saying more than words. Then we went to work quick, helping drive the cattle down to the low meadows.

Later—My eyes are scratchy and I'm tired, but I felt I had to write about this day. I don't think I'll ever forget the beauty of what I saw, but if I did, I would want to have this to read and remember . . . Patrick just brought in another load of wood for me then asked if he could see the flowers he gave me that I'd pressed in the journal. When I showed him, he smiled, satisfied, and said, "And I ain't said bloody once since you told me not to say bloody."

"*Haven't* said," I corrected him, and he grinned up at me, all innocent, his blue eyes twinkling under those thick dark lashes.

"Haven't said bloody," he said.

Sometimes I could swear that Jack and I got our boys "traded" at birth; John-Charles always has his nose stuck in a book when he's not tending the horses . . . and Patrick is so rakish and charming . . . so much like Jack.

Ah, well, Mama said you never pay for your raising

until you have one of your own. But I do have to wonder if I'm not paying Jack's share, too.

So much for poetry.

October 7, 1869 . . .

Patrick came barreling into the cabin tonight, yelling something about "that lady" being here and grabbing my arm until he pulled me out the door, and when I stepped into the yard, I saw it was Willa. She was coming down easy from her wagon, holding a good-sized bundle in her arms, and when she turned around, I saw fear in her eyes as they met mine.

"I found him in between our places, lying off by the side of the trail," she said breathlessly, then she pulled the blanket back to reveal a little Indian boy of about four or five, cuts and bruises all over his face, blood running from his nose and ears. He didn't seem to even have the strength to open his eyes but moaned a pitiful little moan that sounded like a cry for help.

"I don't know anything about children or doctoring," Willa said, her hands shaky as I took the boy from her. "I just assumed you and your family would . . ."

Once we were in the cabin, we made a quick pallet on the floor in front of the fire, and I had Rose go fetch the men. Then Willa and I went to work, trying to clean the blood from his ears and nose and giving him a bit of broth to sip. But he choked and coughed, hardly able to swallow a thing.

Jack got to the cabin first, and it wasn't long after he looked the boy over, studying his wounds first, then his clothes, that he announced the poor little fellow had been beaten by someone. He then told us that his moccasins looked to be Crow, but the beating had probably come from a white as most Indians don't beat their children—or their adults, for that matter.

"Best thing you can do is try to make him comfortable—but he might not make it," Jack said, low, his green eyes filled with pity—and something else, something I couldn't put my finger on as he glanced to where John-Charles was sitting. He left shortly after that to round up the men to follow Willa out and see if they could find anything or anybody around that might tell us who the boy belongs to. Lillie and Jessie came to help, too, but it seems like time will be the only thing to tell if this little one makes it.

I have him bundled on a thick pallet in front of the fireplace as I write this. He has been quiet all night except for just a tiny whimper of a word or two every once in a while in his sleep . . . poor little fellow!

Beaten. Who would do such a thing?

Lord, I won't pretend to understand how this could happen to just a child, but I do ask that You help this little one . . . I pray for his mama, too. I don't understand Crow, but I know the word he calls out every once in a while in his sleep is for his mama.

I know because I'm a mama, too . . .

October 8, 1869 . . .

No news about the boy's family. The children have been such a help, bringing up water from the spring, fetching wood—anything they can do, really. I think they're curious—at least Rose and Patrick are. John-Charles is a different matter, though.

Earlier, I was in my "room" when I heard Patrick and John-Charles bringing in a load of wood for me and the boy started talking again, delirious and mumbling. Then I heard John-Charles say, "What's he sayin'?"

Patrick answered, "Well, *you* should know."

There was a brief silence, then John-Charles said, "No *I* shouldn't, either!"

I heard stomping out of the cabin and came out from behind the curtain to find Patrick standing in the middle of the room with a bewildered look on his face. "I guess I'll stay in here and help, Mama," he said, resigned. "I'll never find John-Charles, anyhow. He always takes off for the woods when he gets mad, and he's been mad all day." He shrugged his shoulders and went over and sat down next to the boy, shaking his head like he didn't know what to make of his cousin.

I wasn't so confused. John-Charles takes after Jack in that way . . . going off to sort out his problems. I think there's a big war going on in that little body—a war of wondering just where he, half-Indian, half-white, fits into this world . . .

Patrick's always had a tender heart, but he has surprised me today at how he's taken it on himself to comfort this poor, sick boy, sitting with him, talking to him, and patting his head like I do when he and Rose are sick. He even got him to take some more broth, though he didn't open his eyes. The boy does seem to sense us sometimes, but he's made no other sound except for the pitiful little word he moans out every once in a while.

I was writing this when I overheard Patrick's voice, coming from somewhere outside the cabin, asking Quinn why anyone would hurt "a little boy like that" and "was it 'cause he's Indian?" There was a short silence that followed, and I knew Quinn was weighing his words. I went and peeked out the window then and saw that Rose and John-Charles were standing there, too. Rose had her arms crossed like she was ready to fight something or somebody, but John-Charles just looked wary, like he wasn't sure he wanted to be there for the answer.

"There is *no* good reason for it, lad," Quinn said, then looked to each of the children. "Folks can say that it's for this reason or that, but 'tis still wrong—in God's eyes and in mine."

"But people still do bad things anyway, don't they?" John-Charles said, then he turned and ran for home before Quinn could answer.

Oh, I hate this trouble, this awful thing that has taken not just one boy's innocence but all of our children's as well.

October 9, 1869 ...

Another day with no news. At least the boy seems to be getting better. He sat up on the pallet today and drank quite a bit of broth then let Patrick show him his collection of bird eggs. His dark eyes were alight with interest until Patrick said "Mama" to me, then his little face crumpled, and he cried until I rocked him back to a fitful sleep.

The wind is picking up in the valley this evening, golden leaves and larch needles swirling everywhere in the air.

October 11, 1869 . . .

Sometimes when I see how quick God works, it amazes me to silence . . . I admit that's an amazing thing in itself, but what has happened is even *more* than that.

Here I prayed for that boy's poor, nameless mother, and Coy trots home tonight with the woman on the back of his horse, her little girl on the back of Jack's mount. Turns out she's the *same* woman we saw in town—same one who's married to that monster, Mr. Carey. She's pretty shook up, her and her daughter both, and wet, too—but they are delirious with joy at finding out the little boy has been in our care all along.

The daughter, Sarah, is about Rose's age and speaks pretty good English. But she's a bit skittish around us.

After hearing all they had been through, I can understand why. It seems Mr. Carey took to beating the little boy something awful the other day, and Willie—that's his name—ran out of their home to get away from his pa, then just kept running. Mother and daughter have been searching for nearly two days and were at their end when Jack and Coy found them near where the stream flows into the river.

"She was out in the river, trying to drown herself and the girl," Jack told us off to one side. "I got off my horse and was trying to talk to her, but she was having none of it at first. Just kept crying and saying she had lost her boy and didn't want to go back home because her husband would beat her and the girl, too. She told me she'd rather die and that it would be better for her daughter to die, too, than to go back home." Jack glanced over at Coy, who was standing in the corner, a bit shy like always. "Then I hear this splash and all of a sudden I see Coy in the water, too, easing out to her and talking to her real gentlelike. She looked shocked to death at first—I don't think she's ever seen a black man—let alone one built like a barn." Coy laughed softly, and Jack shook his head and grinned as he went on. "He don't know Crow, and she don't know much English but something happened because she got out and came with us."

Jack turned and looked at her, listening as she crooned to her little boy. "Wonder how she ever ended up with Carey . . . ," he said almost to himself.

Lillie, Jessie, and me took to the kitchen area so she could be alone with her kids . . . well, that and so we could try and sort out what was happening before our eyes. "For a mother to try and drown herself and her child was more than desperate," Lillie said, whispering.

"Can't imagine what the poor thing has been through," Jessie said, but when she looked at her, there was a knowing despair in Jessie's eyes, like she *could* imagine.

"Makes our lives look like regular picnics, don't it?" Coy said, startling us as we turned to see him standing nearer to us, holding his hat. What startled me most wasn't what he said, for he had just been voicing what we had all been thinking anyway. But it was the look on his face when he turned to watch the woman rocking her boy as Rose tried to coax her girl into playing. Like he was really worried about what might come of her. I saw she was wondering, too, her eyes darting fearfully to the door ever so often. She glanced over at me, and when our eyes met, I had the eeriest feeling that she wasn't in the water anymore—but somehow she was still *drowning*.

I couldn't bare to let her torment go on, so I went to her then and knelt down, asking Jack if he knew what her name was. He said something that sounded like "Awbonny," so I said, "Bonny, you're safe here with us. You're safe—do you know what that means?"

Jack looked doubtful that she'd understand, but she knew, for she looked at me with wide eyes then started to weep with relief.

"Well, I'll be," Jack said as I put my arms around her shoulders.

"Thank . . . you," she said slowly, but as plain as day, and when she raised her eyes, she looked at all of us shyly, gratefully, but she smiled at Coy.

It wasn't too long afterward that Coy offered up his tiny bunkhouse-cabin to "Bonny" and her kids, saying it was only right, being there was just one of him. Our moods lifted a bit until Stem appeared shortly after that. His face was somber with worry as he listened to all that had happened.

"Dern," was all he said at first, taking his hat off and rubbing his head like he did when he was worried. "I got a bad feelin' 'bout this—her bein' Injun and all could spell trouble." We all glanced at Jack—then to Stem, whose look was suddenly sorry. "Didn't mean no offense by that, Jack," he said, gently. "It's jes she ain't got no rights the way most folks see it, if'n he decides to come for her."

Jack nodded, his face grim. "No offense taken," was all he said, but I knew he was thinking of what John-Charles might have to face one day. He looked from Lillie to John-Charles, his green eyes troubled with a distant sorrow, like he was somewhere else. Then he clasped John-Charles's small, brown hand in his, and without another word to any of us, turned as if to walk away. Lillie got up slowly to follow, her own face confused and troubled, and I knew both of them were filled with haunts of the past. When I called after Jack he stopped for only a moment and turned back to me.

"It'll all turn out fine; you'll see," I said, trying in some way to make it better, but he just nodded like his mind was somewhere else.

"I figure we ought to let her stay, at least until we can decide what else to do." Jack glanced over at Stem. "We didn't ask for this . . . but then, neither did she," he added.

When Quinn came in I tried to fill him in the best I could, and he agreed she should stay, too. "But Stem's right about her not having much in the way of rights out here. We're a long way from California, lass," he said, and by the way he said it I knew he meant more than miles . . .

I stepped out only for a moment tonight to see if I could spot Jasper and Honey. That's when I saw Lillie standing off from their little cabin, just looking out toward the mountains. She's small as it is, but she seemed even smaller as I watched her standing alone like that. As I walked over to her, I saw she was holding an empty water bucket in her hand, almost like she had forgot about it. She turned and looked over her shoulder at me, trying to smile.

"Jack's out there somewhere," she said, and that was all she said for a while as I stood next to her, wondering where he'd gone. For as long as I can remember, Jack's always been like that, taking off on his horse whenever he needed to think. "He'll be back," I heard myself tell Lillie, remembering all the times my mama had spoke those same words as I stood with her on our porch in Missouri, watching the distance for Jack. *"It's how he speaks his piece with God,"* Mama had said. *"Some folks take to church, but your brother takes to the land, and it might be he has the right idea about that, too . . ."*

Lillie looked over at me and nodded, then she told me what Jack had said once they got back to the cabin, after he'd tucked John-Charles in for the night. She said he'd looked at her real sad and said, "What kind of life is *my* boy going to have?" She said the "my" part real hard, like she couldn't forget it. I tried to tell her Jack was just worried, that he didn't mean nothing by it, but she just nodded again.

"This land is something, isn't it?" she said after a while, then lowered her voice to a whisper. "You just fall in love with it, whether you should or not." She didn't say any more, but her silence could've filled a book of worry. I knew she wasn't really talking of the land. My feeling, considering all that had happened, was she was thinking of

Jack and John-Charles, who she loved like her very own, and she was wondering where she fit in it all.

I told her that we all felt like that one time or another, that our lives could feel as far out of reach as this land, that the trouble that had happened had got us all feeling low. "We just need to have courage, is all," I finished and was surprised when Lillie looked back over her shoulder at me and smiled, wry. I saw a dimple in her cheek appear, and there was something in the way she cocked her head to one side, in the way her long brown curls straggled free from her bonnet, teased free by the wind, that made me realize how much I loved her like a sister.

"Don't you know, Callie?" she said, like she was laughing at herself as she turned to face the wind again. "Courage is just being the only one who knows you're scared to death."

We both turned back and looked toward the mountains, falling quiet for a spell.

"Well, I guess we blew that, then," I said finally, and we both laughed.

Lillie headed for the spring then, and as I walked back up the trail toward our cabin, a strange feeling stole over me all of a sudden. I felt—even now as I write this—struck by a kind of odd, sad feeling that I just can't shake . . .

October 13, 1869 . . .

Another "casualty" has appeared at our door today. The horse we sold Mr. Carey somehow found its way back here, bearing the telltale signs of being whipped—and whipped hard. Rose was the one who found her. She came running up to the porch where I was, her face streaked with tears, just as Patrick and John-Charles came up from the spring. Overhearing her story, they dropped their pails and ran for the barn. It took some doing, but I finally got them all back to the cabin and quieted down so as not to scare Bonny and her little ones. I found Lillie and Jessie first, then set off to fetch the men, who were out checking cattle. My heart hammered with dread as I rode out.

We decided to meet down at the barn to talk over the latest trouble.

"This place is becoming a regular hospital for Carey's handiwork," Stem said grimly, taking his hat off as he leaned over to take a look at the horse that had been put in a stall by one of the kids. She was lying on her side, panting, but her eyes looked almost human with the same look of relief that had been in Bonny's eyes when she'd looked up at me.

"Bet that sorry excuse was throwed while he was looking for 'em," Stem added.

Quinn was a mile past mad, pacing the barn, trying to figure out what to do, his accent getting thicker by the minute as he talked. "If it weren't for the woman, 'tis sure I'd be payin' the coward a visit, myself."

"Maybe we ought to go ahead and do just that, Quinn," Jack said, his temper getting the better of him. I felt my heart spring up in my chest, fearing the trouble might be enough to turn Jack back to his old ways. "Might be we should just go after him and give him a waylayin' like he did his woman and kids and this here horse."

"No, Jack," I said, not able to keep quiet anymore. "We all came out here to start a new life here. This will blow over. You'll see."

Jack looked doubtful, then Lillie stepped up with a determined look on her face. "You promised, Jack," she said. "We both promised. When we married, we made a promise to God that we'd live our lives different this time. You can't take that promise back just because there's trouble now." Their eyes met, and I saw something in Jack start to give under the weight of Lillie's stare. I was glad to see it.

"Look what He's done for all of us, giving us a new start and all," Lillie added.

"She's right, Jack," Stem said, shocking all of us—even Jessie, who looked as if she'd been suddenly frozen to the spot where she stood. He shook his silver head. "Ain't right t' go back on a promise—especially one t' the Almighty. He ain't played us wrong." Stem set his hat back on his head and looked around at all of us. Then, for some reason, his eyes met mine. "One thing I remember my ol' mama sayin' 'fore she died was, 'Don't give up on Him, an' He won't give up on you. No suh! No matter what it looks like, jes don't give up.'"

"Don't give up," I whispered back, and Stem cocked his head toward me and smiled. His soft smile made me remember all the times he had been there for me—for all of us over the years. A grizzled, old colored man dressed in buckskins, giving a bunch of white folks advice? Who would've ever thought? some people might say. But, again, I knew *Who*. I looked over at Quinn and saw that he knew, too.

"Don't give up," he said, soft, but there was strength in his words, too. Then Lillie was grinning, saying, "Don't give up." Then Coy and Jessie said it, too. Then we all looked to Jack, who stood looking at us like we were crazy but like he needed that kind of crazy more than anything. He took his hat off and ran his hands through his long hair and studied the floor, and I knew there was a war going on in him. A war between the man he was, and the man he wanted to be.

"Don't give up," he said, finally looking up at us, and I saw his eyes were shiny with tears.

I stayed for a while with Jack in the barn, helping him tend to the horse after everyone else had left, thinking it might give us a chance to talk in private. But he was so quiet at first that after he got her up on her feet again I took the salve and went about working it into the mare's hide after Jack cleaned her wounds. He stayed quiet, but I could feel him glance over at me from time to time, and I knew he was weighing his words.

"That was some speech Stem gave," he said after a while. "He was right with what he said—Lillie, too." He looked up at me for a moment, then his eyes went distant with thought. "Doing things the right way is hard, ain't it?" he said, turning back to me. The bewildered tone of his voice made me smile, and I told him I'd thought the same more than once in my life. Jack grinned that grin of his.

"I hope we make it, don't you?" he said then, and I nodded, remembering what Quinn had said to me that long-ago day when Jack had rode away from us, heart-broken, and I had feared I would never see him alive again. *"It's not death he's seeking,"* Quinn had said, understanding Jack more than me. *"It's life . . ."* Now I looked deep in

Jack's eyes and saw the truth of Quinn's words, saw the life-time of yearning and the newness of hope.

"I don't know why, but until all this happened, I'd pretty much put it all out of my mind, you know?" he said, and I knew he meant his life with Raven and the Blackfeet. He shut his eyes tight for a moment, like he was trying to shut out the pain of the memory. "John-Charles thinking of Lillie as his real ma . . . well, I guess it got me thinking it, too. I thought I had to let go of the past so's to have a future. Now I'm wondering if I was right. You know what John-Charles asked me tonight? He asked me if being part Indian made him part bad . . ."

"We're all going to make it, Jack," I told him, trying to swallow past the lump in my throat. "We've got each other. Most of all, we've got the Lord with us."

He looked doubtful for only a moment, then a soft smile came to his face and I saw his eyes go distant with the memory of something. "Believe in the Lord with all your heart and He will save you and your household," he said haltingly, like a baby taking his first steps. "Funny that I'd remember Mama saying that after all these years . . ."

Jack smiled kind of sheepish then and turned back to finish cleaning around the scratches on the mare's neck. The scripture wasn't perfect, but Jack remembering it left me speechless, and I thought of what the preacher had said about God using folks that were broke. I guess I was speechless too long, for I felt Jack swat me with his hat, "Cat got your tongue, sis?" he said. I shook my head and grinned.

"No," I said. "I just had this picture of Mama elbowing Pa up in heaven with that smirk of hers, saying, 'Hear that,

John?' Remember how she used to look so good and pleased when she was right about something?"

Jack grinned wryly. "Yeah, it's about the same look you have on your face right now," he said, and we both laughed.

Lillie and I found the children tonight by way of their voices down at the barn—where they shouldn't have been. As we stepped inside, we could hear the children talking low amongst themselves, then I saw Bonny standing a short distance away, just watching. It wasn't until we came up beside her that we could see what was going on. Willie, still bruised and weak, was standing in the stall with Midnight, his thin arms stretched out as he offered his hand to the horse. I was afraid. But seeing the two together was like nothing I'd ever witnessed. Even John-Charles, who had an uncanny bond with horses, knew it was something special, for he, Rose, and Patrick kept their distance and just watched.

Midnight's ears flickered, then she sniffed the air and finally staggered over to the boy. With great gentleness, the horse began to nuzzle him, touching on each of his bruises with her velvet muzzle, like she was comforting his hurts. And he did the same, softly running his fingers over her scratches and scrapes, with a tenderness that brought tears to my eyes. It was as if they knew they had both suffered by the same hand, and it had forged a bond between them.

"I ain't ever saw a horse do that," Patrick said. Bonny said something in her own language that sounded like an answer. Patrick glanced to John-Charles for his take on it, but he just shrugged.

"Horses ain't like people. They have sense," Rose said with a sniff. "I'm gonna ask Pa if I can keep her now." Lillie and I grinned at each other then turned to Bonny, who had been watching her son and the horse with as much amazement as the rest of us.

"You look like Willie, kinda," Patrick said suddenly, looking at John-Charles, "'Cept for your eyes are green like Uncle Jack's. I wonder if your ma looked like Miss Bonny." Patrick just wasn't able to let go of his curiosity over his cousin being part Indian, especially now that another half-Indian boy was there to look at. I glanced over at Lillie, who suddenly looked like she had been struck.

"I know what my ma looks like . . . ," John-Charles started to say as he turned around. Then he stopped in his tracks, seeing Lillie and me standing there, and he smiled. "She's right over there," he pointed at Lillie, then ran headlong into her arms, hugging her around the waist. Lillie grinned at me with big tears in her eyes.

"Well, yes, I *am* your ma," Lillie said, petting his head. "But you had another ma, too. So that means you've been loved double, and there's not many people can say that." The happy way John-Charles looked up at Lillie made me wish Jack was there to witness it, and I couldn't help smiling, too.

It was as if in spite of all the trouble, we were being fit together, piece by piece . . . like the giant hand of Providence was putting the puzzle of our lives back into place.

"Good family," Bonny said, smiling at us.

I have to agree.

Quinn says Coy has planted himself in a tent outside his bunkhouse, and that when he rode by, he saw Coy sitting just outside the flap of the tent, cleaning his gun. I asked why he'd be there, even though I knew deep down that, without being asked, Coy had quietly accepted the job of protector over Bonny and her kids. Quinn smiled at me tenderly, and I knew he was thinking of when we first met and how he'd watched over me and my baby sister, over all our family, like we had always been his.

"A man can't help but want to protect those he cares for," he said. "Even if he isn't sure where it will lead him."

I hugged him tight, wishing I could stay wrapped in his big, comforting arms like that forever and wondering where those feelings would lead Coy . . . would lead us all . . .

October 15, 1869 . . .

Cold and windy today. The men are keeping an eye out for Mr. Carey as they bring strays back down from the high country. I feel like we're teetering on the edge of something happening, but I'm not sure what. Willa came to call earlier as I was packing up the noon meal for Coy to take out to the rest of the men.

"Something's happened, hasn't it?" she said, nearly running Coy over as she came through the door. Coy tipped his hat as he walked out, but she hardly noticed as she rushed on. "I had the strangest feeling I was being watched the whole drive over. It's too quiet, too. Where are your kids . . . where's the boy?"

I told her everything then, about the woman showing up with her daughter, how she'd been so filled with despair over everything that had happened she'd nearly taken her own life and her girl's, too. Then I told her about the horse showing up and how it had taken to the boy, even comforting him, and I saw tears fill her eyes—even though she was quick to blink them back.

"They've been through too much," I said. "We don't have any other choice but to help them."

"Oh, there is always another choice," she said, standing to her feet again. "There is the choice to stay out of the way of Jed Carey. He's not just a drunk—he's a dangerous drunk." She must have saw the stubbornness on my face, for she sat back down with a great sigh.

"Lunatics," she declared, then she bit her lip and looked at me.

"So, what can I do to help?"

October 16, 1869 . . .

True to her word, Willa has just come from town today with news of Mr. Carey, and we are not sure what to make of it. According to Mr. Audrey, Jed Carey is going around telling everyone that his wife's *people* "came like skunks in the night and made off with her, his kids, and his best horse."

"He's making quite a show of it, too," Willa said, standing in the yard with us all, "even going as far as saying he would pay a reward to get them back."

"He'll be gettin' a *reward* of his own when the good Lord gets a'holt of him," Jessie said, planting her hands upon her hips.

Stem chuckled, pulling her close to wrap his arms around her. "He surely wouldn't want to tangle with my Jess here. She's pret' near a force to be reckoned with herself," he said, then laughed again as she tried to shoo him away while looking pleased, herself.

"Why do you suppose he's made up such a tale?" Jack asked, dismounting. He wiped the dust from his face with the rag Lillie handed him then looked out to where the children were all playing together. We all looked. Bonny sat on the ground in front of the cabin, sewing contentedly on the goods she'd scrounged from us. For someone who had no real home, she looked so happy, so grateful, and I think every one of us felt the bittersweetness of it.

"He said it 'cause he's got somethin' up his sleeve, thet's why," Stem said. "Only conscience that feller has is when someone is lookin'. I know we ain't supposed to question God's creation, but a person does have to wonder sometimes . . ."

"We ain't gonna send her back," Coy said, then looked at all of us. "She has a right to *live*, don't she?" When he looked away from us all, I knew it was so he could try to hide his emotions.

"That boy was almost dead when Willa brought him here," Quinn said. "They were all almost dead. I don't think I could sleep, knowin' I sent them back to be finished off."

"Maybe it will all blow over," Willa said, but her face was doubtful, and so was Jack's. I saw it in his eyes mostly, how they were turned down at the corners that made him look so different than the Jack I had stood laughing with in the barn only a couple of days ago.

"Ma'am," he said to Willa then, shaking his head, "there's been a lot I've gambled on in my life. I'm not a betting man no more, but even if I was, I wouldn't bet on *that*."

October 19, 1869 . . .

Jack was right about it not blowing over. Jeb Carey showed up at the ranch this morning, full of the devil himself.

Coy had spotted him as he was riding through the upper pasture and came racing to the cabins to warn us all. There was just enough time, thank the Lord, for Jessie to get Bonny and her children hidden away inside before he came trotting up. He spotted Midnight standing in one of the corrals, and I watched as he dismounted and fairly stomped to the fence where Jack, Quinn, and Stem were standing. They talked low at first, but I saw it was quickly getting heated, and I felt my heart come up clear to my throat. I started praying over and over, *Please Lord, just let him leave,* when I heard Stem say, "No, you ain't, either." Then I saw Jack hand him money, saw Mr. Carey throw the money on the ground.

"Thieves! I bought that horse fair and square," Mr. Carey hollered, and I could see the muscle in Jack's jaw jump clear from where I was standing. Then Mr. Carey started looking around, his gaze going to where Coy's cabin stood, and Lillie said under her breath, "Oh, please, God."

Coy came around the side of the corrals with his rifle, and I felt my heart drop. He said, "We don't want no trouble, mister, so you best git now." He picked the money up and tried to hand it to Mr. Carey, who looked at Coy like he was crazy.

"I ain't takin' nothin' from you, *boy*," Mr. Carey said, then Quinn took the money from Coy and handed it to Mr. Carey, the sound of his voice deadly calm.

"We don't deal with folks who mistreat their animals," Quinn said. "'Twould be best if you take your leave now."

Mr. Carey glanced back to his horse, and when I saw him eye his own rifle I ducked my head quick to pray, "Please Lord, You can't let this happen, not after we've come all this way."

I heard Lillie say "Amen" softly, and when I opened my eyes I saw her knuckles were white from squeezing the porch rail so hard. We watched Mr. Carey eye the men for a tense moment, then he got back on his horse.

"Horse thieves are hung in these parts, in case you don't know," Jeb Carey said, wheeling his horse around one last time to face Quinn.

"Maybe you should remember that, in case you think to come here again," Quinn said evenly. "There's nothing here that belongs to you anymore."

Mr. Carey rode off, and as soon as we saw he was gone, Lillie and I headed for Coy's cabin. It was dark inside so we couldn't see nothing at first, but then Jessie, seeing it was us, lit a lamp, and we saw Bonny and Sarah over in the corner, tears rolling down their faces as they hunched over Willie, trying to calm his shaking.

"Lord forgive me for sayin' it, but I think I would have fought him with my bare hands if he'd come in here and tormented these folks again," Jessie said, looking up at us with an aching sadness in her eyes . . .

Willa came back tonight, and after hearing all that happened, she shook her head then walked over to where Bonny was sitting in front of my fireplace.

She eyed Bonny close—and Bonny eyed her, too—and I saw something pass between them, like a silent understanding of sorts.

"It might be best if Bonny and her children came to stay with me for a while," she said, more a statement than a question. Much to our surprise, Bonny readily accepted the offer. So, with heavy hearts, we helped them pack up what little they had acquired since they'd come to our place. Rose, Patrick, and John-Charles were angry, then forlorn, as their new friends climbed into Willa's wagon. Bonny hugged each one of us then surprised the children by giving them each a pair of moccasins she had made special for them.

We were all near tears. Somehow, without our really realizing it, Bonny and her children had become like family. Even the men went over to the wagon to say their good-byes. Bonny politely shook all of their hands— except for Coy. Shyly she offered him the necklace she had been wearing, reaching up gently to put it around his thick neck then turning quick to climb in the wagon. Willa watched us all with something akin to wonder on her face.

"I've never seen people care so much for folks like your family does," she said, accepting Quinn's hand to help her climb up onto the wagon seat next to Bonny. "It sure makes a person wonder . . ."

She didn't finish the thought but hawed the team on. When I turned to walk away, I saw Coy standing off to one side by himself, watching them leave with a tumble of emotions in his dark, thoughtful eyes. He didn't say anything but just watched until they were long out of sight. Suddenly that verse of Longfellow's played through my mind:

He speaketh not; and yet there lies, a conversation in his eyes. . . .

I had just got Rose and Patrick to bed (wearing their moccasins) and set down to write this when I overheard the men talking outside.

"'Been my experience that hard-boiled eggs are mostly yeller on the insides," I heard Stem saying, and I knew they were talking of Mr. Carey.

"You might be right," Jack said after a while, "but I still have a bad feeling about him leavin' so easy. There's something your pa told me awhile back, Coy, and I ain't ever forgot it."

"What's that?" I heard Coy say.

Jack cleared his throat then, and I heard him answer, "Never trust a wolf 'til it's been skinned."

Quinn must have showed up about then, because I heard his voice, then I heard them all moving away.

Oh, how I wish this trouble hadn't come to our door!

Lord, I can't say I understand why all of this has happened, just when we thought we were through with the bad times for a while. I would be lying if I said I did understand, and I know You aren't keen on liars, so I'll just ask You to please help us. Mama told me more than once that trials come to test our faith, but I recall her saying, too, that You always light our way through the darkness. Seeing the worried look on everyone's faces, and now, hearing what I just did . . . I pray Your help comes soon.

October 22, 1869 . . .

It's come as no surprise to us that Coy's decided to stay in Willa Cain's bunkhouse, as restless as he's been the past few days. "Ain't good for them ladies to be alone out there like that," he told us, shaking his head worriedly as he packed up after dinner. Jack told me once that Coy, like his pa, was the type to walk through fire for those he cared for. Selfless to a fault, is how he described him.

"You're a good man, Coy Harper," I said suddenly, and he turned and looked at me with a kind of surprised smile on his face. Then before he could say anything I ran up and hugged him, whispering I'd be praying for him.

"Why, I guess I'd appreciate that 'bout more than any-thing," he said, tipping his hat and smiling shyly before he mounted his horse.

Watching him ride away, I didn't know quite how to feel. I think Quinn sensed my uneasiness because he walked over to where I was standing and put his arm around me, smiling gently. "Everything's going to work out, Callie. You'll see," he said. I felt better just having him there, like everything wasn't so bad after all.

"It's a good thing seein' that young feller doin' fer 'em like he is," Stem said wistfully. "Makes an old man feel real shiny 'bout things agin."

I looked over at Jack and Lillie then and saw them smile at each other.

"Ye feel that shiny, I guess ye can get down to our cabin

and finish that quilt frame for me," Jessie said, and Stem shook his head.

"Why, Jess, ye just took the poetry out of the moment," Stem said, grinning, and we all laughed. The laughter sounded so good.

Maybe things *will* get back to normal . . . A person can hope, at least, can't she?

October 24, 1869 . . .

Sabbath. Too bad we haven't heard any news about Preacher. I'm not that keen on going to town right now, but I think it would do me a world of good to hear one of his sermons—do us *all* a world of good.

November 1, 1869 . . .

It's a good thing we had Bonny and the kids go to Willa's. Mrs. Audrey came to call today with her fellow "sufferettes," as Rose calls them, and I have a feeling they would've fairly *ran* back to town with the news if they'd found Bonny here, the way they carried on about "poor Mr. Carey" at first.

Lillie, Jessie, and me were sitting on the new porch, watching the children play, when we saw the wagon with Mrs. Audrey and her twins coming our way, followed by another wagon and a buggy. Rose glanced up then stood like a startled rabbit, spotting Mrs. Audrey. Then she got a considering look on her face when she saw the twins were with her, like she was thinking the trouble of tolerating Mrs. Audrey just might be worth it for a chance to have some playmates. She and the boys watched warily as Mrs.

Audrey stepped down followed by a smallish woman, dressed poor but tidy, in the other wagon, then an older, plumpish woman who groaned loudly as she stepped from her buggy. The buggy leaned dangerously sideways as she lowered her bulk to the ground, and I saw Rose, Patrick, and John-Charles's heads lean with it as they watched. I quickly called for them, suggesting they take the twins to see the new foal down at the barn.

Mrs. Audrey was the first to reach us. "Mrs. McGregor," she said, nodding to me and then to Lillie and Jessie, "Mrs. Pumphrey, Mrs. Spence, and I thought it would be nice for us ladies to get togeth-uh—since there ah so few of us out he-ah."

"What I thought was I would be bored to death if I didn't get out of my house," the plumpish woman said, huffing past Mrs. Audrey. "I'm Mrs. Pumphrey. Do you mind if I sit a spell?" Mrs. Audrey pursed her lips, and Mrs. Spence didn't say anything at all. Jessie and me went and fetched the chairs from around the table, and we no more than got seated on the porch when the talk began.

"I suppose you've *hud* 'bout po-ah Mr. Carey losin' his wife and little ones?" Mrs. Audrey said, then went on before any of us could answer. "Just a puh-fect tragedy. He is offerin' a reward, you know, though I don't suppose it would have to be much—I've heard savages like that can be bribed for next to *nuth-*in'."

I thought it odd that they didn't know of "poor Mr. Carey's" visit to our place the day before, but I didn't say anything. Mrs. Spence cleared her throat and looked pointedly at Mrs. Audrey then tilted her head slightly toward Lillie.

"Oh, Delia, Mr. Wade was *captured* by them—that doesn't make him one," Mrs. Audrey said, then turned to look at Lillie. "Isn't that right, Mrs. Wade?" But before Lillie could ask what they were talking about, Mrs. Pumphrey leaned toward me.

"It's a pure wonder your brother turned out as well as he did," she said, shaking her head. "I mean, to be captured by Indians at such a young age! Then those years with the wolf pack—how did he ever manage to find you again, dear?"

It wasn't until that very moment that I realized Jack had done more than get our supplies for us that day in the mercantile. I honestly think I heard my whole family turning over in their graves. "It was surely a miracle," I said, thinking it *would* be a miracle if he wasn't struck by lightning for lying. I tried not to look at Lillie, who was coughing—or laughing—into her handkerchief. Jessie rose abruptly, saying how she had to "go check something," and I saw her shoulders shake as she went out through the door.

"Well, what I would like to know is, how did he *ev*-uh learn English?" Mrs. Audrey said.

"Oh, he always has had a way with words," I said. At least *that* wasn't a lie. Lillie got up and fetched the ginger cakes I'd made earlier while I brought out the coffee, but neither of us looked at each other for fear of laughing. Jessie stayed absent—and I'm glad now she did, the way the conversation turned then.

"You have quite a spread here," Mrs. Pumphrey started, taking a healthy bite of cake. "I imagine it takes a lot of work, though."

"A wise decision to bring yo-ah pee-ple along," Mrs.

Audrey sniffed. "I'd have one of my own if Mr. Audrey would just relent."

"Stem, Jessie, and Coy are *not* our servants, Mrs. Audrey," I said, unable to put up with her hateful ways any longer. "They own their home and part of this land, too, just like we do—we're all *partners.*"

"Well, I nev-uh *hud* of such a thing!" Mrs. Audrey said, her cheeks turning pink. I saw her glance over to Mrs. Spence, who looked like she had sunk so far back in the rocking chair she might disappear any moment.

"Well, the war *is* over, Leah," Mrs. Pumphrey allowed, taking another ginger cake.

A commotion caused our heads to turn as the children came running around the corner of the house, piling in, hungry and dirty. Mrs. Audrey's twins, Zora and Nora, looked happy until they saw the horrified look on their mother's face. "What have you two . . . ," she started to say.

"Why, he looks a lot like Mr. Carey's boy," Mrs. Pumphrey said, eying John-Charles, but Mrs. Spence "reappeared" from the rocking chair long enough to elbow her.

"This is *my* son, John-Charles," Lillie said then, and I could see she had had her fill of the women, too. She put her arm around his shoulder protectively and looked straight into each woman's eyes like she was daring them to say another thing. I couldn't help thinking that her claiming him out loud like that had done something good for her. Something good for both of them.

The ladies' eyes went from Lillie to John-Charles and back to Lillie again as if trying to figure it out.

"Ma'am," John-Charles said politely to each one of

them, dipping his head in a gentlemanly bow just like he'd been taught.

Patrick grinned, standing next to him. "His grandpa is a *med-cin* man," he announced proudly.

"Enough said," Mrs. Audrey announced, rising abruptly as she and the ladies quickly said their good-byes. The twins were the only ones of the bunch who looked sad to leave.

"Enough said!" I repeated sternly, then I turned back to Lillie. "First time since I met that woman that we agree on anything."

As the women climbed up into their wagons and buggy, Lillie smiled at me, but in her eyes I saw a fleeting look of hurt that she tried to hide. We watched the kids run back out the door in silence, then she turned to me again. "Why do people act like that, Callie? Like you have to be a certain way or you just don't measure up. I never have understood it," she said, shaking her head.

"I don't think God understands it, either," I said, watching the dust clouds swirl behind the departing women. Then I thought and added, "But He does say to pray for those that hurt you."

"He really says that?" Lillie said with such an earnest but worried look on her face, I had to chuckle.

"Yes, He really does," I said. "But I don't think He'd mind us asking for the strength to do it." Lillie looked at me for a long moment, then squared her shoulders.

"Well, let's pray for some strength, then," she said, and we both grinned at each other like young girls as we joined hands.

"Well, will ye look at all them teeth," Jessie said, announcing her return from her cabin. Then she must've realized why we were standing like we were, for she looked suddenly sheepish. "I guess I missed more than I thought," she added, then came and joined us in our "strengthening" prayer.

The men thought it was the funniest thing they'd ever heard when we told them over dinner what the ladies from town had said about Jack. They laughed, shook their heads, then laughed again.

I admit it was good to hear them laugh. But I did try my best to look fierce, telling Jack it wasn't the Christian thing to do, making up outlandish stories about our family and all.

"Aw now, sis," Jack said, wiping the tears from his eyes from laughing so hard. "I didn't mean nothin' by it—I just figured they'd be so busy tryin' to figure out my story, they wouldn't have time to pick on no one else." He looked over at Quinn and Stem and winked. "Like I said earlier, we're all in this together, ain't we?"

"What's this *we?*" Stem said, unable to hide the smile on his old face. "Ye got a tapeworm in there with ye?"

We all laughed at that, then talk soon turned to the ranch and what work still had to be done before winter set in for good. Stem, Jack, and Quinn took their leave not long after, to finish up with the cattle before nightfall, and we women had set to doing the dishes when Rose pulled on my skirt to get my attention.

"I asked Nora, Mama," Rose told me, her voice like a whisper as she dried one of the dishes. When I asked her what she meant, she winced and put her finger to her lips like it was a grave secret.

"I asked Nora if their mother was from the *plains*," she said with her usual flair. I looked at Lillie and Jessie, who were smiling as they dried dishes, too.

"Aw, Rose, Zora said it ain't so. She said her mama ain't a Long *or* from the plains," Patrick said, looking up from his game of marbles with John-Charles. He shook his head. "Their pa just got her in the mail, is all."

"You weren't supposed to tell," John-Charles said, looking up with a frown.

"The *mail?*" Lillie, Jessie, and me said at the same time, and Patrick shook his head at us, too.

"He-ordered-her-in-the-mail," he said then, sounding out each word slowly like he was talking to a child. "From the United of States."

"Why, he means she was a mail-order bride," Jessie said, a wide grin breaking out over her face. She winked at Lillie, who was looking a bit relieved to not have to worry about "measuring up" so much.

"Now, honey, that is news sure enough. But it *still* don't beat being kidnapped or raised by wolves," she said wryly, and we all laughed.

Stem just told me that he stopped by Willa's to "check up on things." He said Willa had went to town for supplies and Mr. Audrey just so happened to mention that the blacksmith had up and closed his shop along about noon and told Mr. Audrey he wasn't sure when he would be coming back—or if he would.

Oh, I pray that man is gone for good. We could sure use the peace.

November 2, 1869 . . .

We woke this morning to find the windows iced over with thick fingers of frost tempting us outside for a look. Opening the door brought a bitter wind, sweeping Jasper and Honey in with it, looking relieved, then confused, as Quinn and I stepped outside, shutting the door behind us, sharing a cup of coffee and the silence. It felt like we hadn't been alone in months, so we talked. About little things, really: the cattle, the horses, how they'd fare when winter set in . . . we talked about things we'd like to do to the cabin next spring.

When we fell quiet again, it was like we were still talking, but in a different way. We just stood looking at everything—the valley, the mountains, the sky—and I couldn't help thinking how close we'd become in spite of the work, in spite of even the trouble—or maybe it was because of it.

The door flew open shortly after that moment, and Patrick and Rose stared out at us much like Jasper and Honey had stared *in* at us as they shivered in the cold.

"What are ya lookin' at?" Patrick asked, and Quinn smiled at me before looking over his shoulder.

"Old Man Winter is coming," Quinn said, and I saw Rose and Patrick look up at him then peer out the door, past the yard.

"I don't see no old man," Patrick said, and we chuckled, turning to go back inside.

Rose laughed, too, like she understood, but I saw her take one last look before she shut the door. Just in case.

Promiseland

Stem just finished attaching the ropes to our cabins, linking us together so we won't get lost in the snow that Jack says is sure to come soon. I was sitting on the porch, taking a short break despite the cold, and was struck by the sweetness of Stem and Rose's talk, so I thought I'd write it down—if my fingers don't freeze in the meantime.

"Brains in the head saves blisters on the feet," I heard him say as Rose followed close on his heels while he nailed his end of the sturdy rope to each cabin. "Or frostbite on the toes, I shoulda said."

Rose giggled.

"But it's not snowing *yet,*" she added, and he nodded, cocking his old head to one side as he looked at her.

"An' it weren't raining when ol' Noah built his ark, either, sis," he said. "That be lesson number seven hundred ninety-nine, I'm thinkin'. Do ye know what it means?"

Rose's chin tilted up in nine-year-old indignation. "Of course I do," she said. "It means you get ready for something that's coming instead of waiting 'til it's too late."

Stem conceded then. "Well, it's a good thing yer smart," he said, and Rose beamed up at him. Stem smiled, too, as he finished tacking the last of the rope. Then I watched him reach down and gently take Rose's hand in his.

"If I had a daughter I'd wish her to be smart like you," he said, and I saw Rose look up at him thoughtfully, saw her eyes go tender all of a sudden.

"I can be your daughter, too, Stem," Rose said. "I know my pa wouldn't mind sharing. He's real good like that."

I felt tears spring to my eyes then, and though I couldn't see Stem as he and Rose headed off toward Stem and Jessie's cabin to fasten the other end of the rope, I knew he must've had tears in his eyes, too. I heard him clear his throat a bit and say, "Well, yer right about yer pa bein' good, sis."

My cold fingers feel raw and sore as I write this. I have cleaned, cooked, and cleaned again today, and I just finished my mending. I'm tired to the bone, but I can't *not* write.

It's times like these I never want to forget.

Just when I think Rose is one person, she surprises me once again. Tonight she proved it by presenting us with her finished sampler after dinner. It says

> For my mama.
> One thing I know:
> I hatd evry stich I sode.
> But I love my mama,
> Pa and evin Patrik to.

It was all we could do not to laugh—Quinn almost undid me, trying to look so sober and thoughtful as he studied her work—which was surprisingly neat—but all the time laughter lighting his blue eyes.

We *did* laugh after she went off to bed, then Quinn went out to the barn and promptly made a little frame for it. I have hung it next to a sampler I did when I wasn't yet fifteen. It says

How does the meadow flower its bloom unfold?
Because the lovely little flower is free
   down to its root,
  and in that freedom, bold.

Quinn says they're a fitting pair. And I can't help but agree.

November 17, 1869 . . .

Slow morning. We've been working so hard around here to get ready for winter that I've hardly had time to take a breath. Purple-looking clouds hanging over the valley seem to bring a stillness to the air that no one can figure. It's not just the cold, but something about its looks that feels like winter.

The men have set out to try and find a wild turkey—or two. Jessie says the way they rode out of here you'd think they were desperate for something besides beef . . .

I best put this pen to rest now. There is so much to do for tomorrow!

November 25, 1869 . . .
Thanksgiving Day

And such a good day it's been, too. I feel like everything has finally settled down, no whispers or signs of Mr. C (I don't even like writing his name). Coy drove the wagon over here to bring Willa, Bonny, and the kids, and we had a fine time of it, everybody hugging or shaking hands like we hadn't seen each other in forever. The kids even got in on the hand-shaking, which sent them into a fit of giggles. They bundled up not long after and took off outside to play while we moved the furniture back and set up a long plank table in front of the fireplace that I covered with a linen tablecloth to spruce things up a bit. Then the men went to fetch more chairs from the other cabins to seat our "guests."

By the time they got back, with all the little ones trailing in behind them, we had the whole center length of the table covered with fixings. Everyone had brought something to share, so there was more than plenty. The men had given up on finding turkeys, but they supplied plenty of meat, just the same. We had roasted antelope, roasted sage hen, and—imagine!—roasted rabbit. There was beans and squash. Jessie made the gooseberry sauce, and Lillie surprised us with apple dumplings she'd made out of dried apples.

Stem, being the oldest of the group, said grace, his voice filled with great emotion. Surely there wasn't a more grateful group to say "amen" and mean it, than us. Even Bonny seemed to understand what our thanks meant as she cast a look at each of us, tears in her eyes. Willa tried to appear casual about the whole thing, but I could see she was touched, too.

Everything was so good—the food, the fire crackling in the fireplace, the laughter bursting out in all directions— that for a moment I wanted to weep, wanted us all to stay just the way we were. But too soon we were clearing the first of the dishes away while everyone complained about eating too much but kept eying the desserts anyway.

Willa, with her notorious sweet tooth, had brought two pies *and* one of the lushest cakes I'd ever seen. Quinn said it made his teeth hurt just to look at it, but that didn't stop him from going back for seconds, saying he was, "storing up for winter." Coy seconded the idea, and Willa, standing between the two, just shook her head, saying she felt like she was in the "land of the giants."

Stem struck up a lively tune on his fiddle soon after and had the children dancing a little jig as we clapped for them, laughing until our bellies ached at their antics. Then Stem played a sweet tune for Jessie, so haunting and pretty. I thought it sounded familiar, but I couldn't place where I'd heard it before. I mentioned a few tunes, trying to guess, then gave up.

"'Course ye ain't heard it. I jes made it up," Stem said smugly with a twinkle in his rheumy eyes. "'Ode to Jessie,' it's called."

Jessie beamed a smile at Stem, and he took up the fiddle and started playing again.

"You trying to make the rest of us look bad or something?" Jack said, and Stem grinned.

"Ain't no tryin' to it," he said, and we all laughed. "Ye get as old as I am, ye better have learned at least one thing well."

"Gettin' old ain't so bad, if I handle it as good as you," Jack said.

Stem thought for a moment then answered, "Only one drawback I know of t' bein' old. An' thet's havin' sech a young memory."

"What's wrong with that?" Quinn asked, smiling.

"Why, bein' able to remember thet my body once *fit* the memory," Stem said, like it should have been obvious, and we all laughed again.

"I'm glad I met ye when ye was older," Jessie said, shaking her head. "I don't think I'd been able to put up with ye as a youngster."

"I'd a jes been fightin' the swarm of beaus tryin' to get at ye," Stem said. Jessie sniffed, but we could all tell she was pleased. Then I saw Jack look at Lillie, and I felt that odd twinge of sadness again, knowing the night was starting to end as he scooped up John-Charles's sleeping little form off the pallet in front of the fireplace. Rose and Patrick never moved a muscle when Coy went to pick up Bonny's little ones and carry them to the wagon.

Outside, Willa hugged me tighter than usual. "You take care of that family of yours, you hear," she said stepping up into the wagon.

Coy, taking extra care to help Bonny into the wagon, didn't go unnoticed by us, either. Quinn and I watched Jessie and Stem walk hand in hand back to their cabin, then he put his arm around my shoulders as we took a quick stroll back into the house.

"You'd think it was spring and not winter coming, with all this love in the air," Quinn said. I grinned up at him.

"So, the honeymoon *isn't* over yet, then?" I said, and we both chuckled.

"'Tis far from over," Quinn said after a while. Then, before we stepped back inside, he hugged me to him, wrapping his arms around me to warm me and maybe to blot out the world for a while, so it could be just me and him.

"Would God that it would always feel like this for us, lass," he whispered in my ear, and there was such a wistful note to his voice. Then he said, "Look at that," pointing to the moon that seemed to hang, bold and bright, just above the tops of the mountains, looking so big and close that it awed me—and scared me a little, too.

Every time I've thought I had a handle on this land, it overwhelms me with its grandeur, making me feel small again and unsure . . . almost like the feeling of holding a newborn in my arms for the very first time. One minute I'm so awed by the gift from God, so in love . . . then, the next minute, I'm scared to death I've been given too big a test to pass.

I almost told Quinn what I was feeling, but when I looked up at him, he was still looking at the moon. "Sometimes it doesn't seem real, does it?" he said then. "It doesn't seem possible this is our *home* now." He leaned over and kissed me so tenderly I lost what I was going to say . . .

November 26, 1869 . . .

Strange weather this afternoon. The sun shone bright while a heavy rain fell down over the valley. Some of the cattle hightailed it up the slopes for the woods, and the men had to fight to bring them down again.

By the time I went to fetch some more water from the stream this evening, it had turned bitter cold. Quinn said they could feel their own sweat freezing on them as they drove the cattle back down the mountain.

During dinner indoors tonight the men barely lasted through the meal as tired as they all are. I read Rose, Patrick, and John-Charles the "fiery furnace story," as Patrick calls it, and could barely keep my eyes open to finish. Lord help me, but I'm not done yet. Mending to finish tonight before I shut my eyes . . .

November 28, 1869 . . .

Cold, cold day.

I found Stem down at the stream when I went to fetch the water this morning. He was just sitting on the bank with his silver head cocked sideways, his breath coming out in slow streams of steam as he studied the mountains and the sky beyond. Something about the way he looked touched my heart, made me remember, too, the nights he'd sat up with me on the trail and told me stories about his life. He must have sensed me, for he suddenly turned and looked.

"I declare, I was fixed t' thinkin' I'd seen it all, 'fore I seen this here spread, Callie," he said, motioning toward the mountains and the thick clouds suspended above them. When he turned to me I saw that there was a serious but kind look to his rheumy old eyes as he smiled. "Get as old as I am, an' ya start wonderin' if all there is to see has done been seen. Good thing t' find out there's still good land *and* good people t' be knowed before yer lamp gets blowed out."

He struggled to his feet then and took the pails from me, filling them for me, "so as not to freeze them purty hands," he said. As I watched him bend over, slow and stiff like that, it was if I suddenly noticed how old he really was, how thin his shoulders looked, how the shock of silver hair seemed wispier, how his old, leathered face looked frailer as he turned back toward me. Slowly I felt something like fear fill me. Why hadn't I noticed it all before? I thought.

"I think your lamp has plenty of light left, if you ask me," I said, trying to joke past the lump in my throat. Stem chuckled, and the sound of his laugh made me feel a bit better. Watching him dip his own pails into the water, I felt myself shiver a bit.

"Ya got that right, Callie," he said with a sudden mischievous glint to his eye. "Lots left to do—ol' Jess's quilt frame fer one thing. If'n I don't get it finished soon . . . well, I don't think heaven itself could hide me from that kind of wrath," he added, and we both grinned, walking up the path to our cabins.

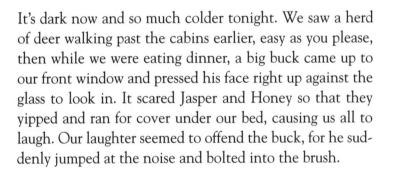

It's dark now and so much colder tonight. We saw a herd of deer walking past the cabins earlier, easy as you please, then while we were eating dinner, a big buck came up to our front window and pressed his face right up against the glass to look in. It scared Jasper and Honey so that they yipped and ran for cover under our bed, causing us all to laugh. Our laughter seemed to offend the buck, for he suddenly jumped at the noise and bolted into the brush.

November 30, 1869 . . .

Another cold day. The thick layer of frost this morning upset Stem's horse as he was heading out to check on the cattle and sent him tumbling, scaring Jessie half to death—scaring us all. Stem just laughed it off. "I got more lives than a cat, Jess, ye ought t' know that by now," he said and got right back up on his horse.

Best close for now. The wood box is getting low again, and I still have some baking to do.

Later—We had no more than laid our heads down when a hard wind picked its way through the valley, moaning against the cabins. The noise got louder, and all of a sudden I felt the cabin shudder. Quinn and I sat up at the same time, then we heard Lillie's frightened voice come from way off shrieking, "Jack, where's John-Charles?" We scrambled then, throwing our clothes on, lighting lanterns. Rose was standing in her shift with the cabin door wide open when we got to her.

"Look, Mama," she said, her voice hushed with awe. We followed her gaze in shocked silence as we looked upon the herd of wild horses huddled amongst our cabins. Then we saw John-Charles, plain as day, right in the middle of the herd, holding his hand out to one of the horses, smiling.

"I'll distract them, Jack," Quinn called. "You grab the boy."

Quinn eased himself out the door as Stem appeared and headed for the opposite side of the herd. Strange enough, the wild horses didn't seem the least bit frightened. We all watched them in awe as they pawed the ground, throwing their heads back and snorting puffs of steam as if to let us know they had laid claim to the yard.

"Dern if they don't act like we're the ones trespassin'," I heard Stem say, and for some reason the sound in his voice made me uneasy.

Jack finally got ahold of John-Charles while Quinn and Stem worked for nearly another hour, trying to run the horses off from the cabins by waving their arms and coaxing them to go instead of having to use their guns and startle our own herds.

The uneasiness that settled over me when I first saw the horses has stayed with me tonight as I write this. I get these kinds of feelings sometimes. My mama and her mama before her had feelings about things, too. Mama used to say it was just God giving His children notice about things, but I'm not exactly sure what this feeling means . . .

I just wish I knew . . .

I decided to take a walk after everyone else went back to bed tonight since I couldn't get to sleep. I couldn't help thinking of Stem's words as I looked out across the valley, and I did feel like a trespasser for some reason, felt like maybe it wasn't our promiseland after all and those mustangs had every right to resent us.

Are we supposed to be here? I asked the land—asked God.

I didn't get an answer. But as I hugged the blanket around my shoulders, feeling the bite in the air that promised the snow to come, I knew the land would have its say before it answered my question.

And so would God . . .

Oh, this beautiful, awful land . . . Lord, how can I love something and, now, fear it, too?

> *Why art thou cast down, O my soul?*
> *and why art thou disquieted within me? . . .*
> —PSALM 42:11

PART TWO

Out of the Wilderness

Then the peple got scairt an forgot everthing. They evin forgot wich way they was goin and got lost in the wilderness. Moses liftd his arm agin and askd God to show them The Way. And God did.

By Rose McGregor
age 9 1/2
Mountana Teritery, 1869

I feel like we woke up in a different land today. It's almost *balmy* outside, the big, wide sky so blue it doesn't seem real after the days of cloudy, snow-choked sky and chilled wind. Jack says it's a *Chinook* wind but that the miners back in Virginia City called it the *fickle lady* because it blows into your life one minute, all sunny and warm, and the next, it leaves you back out in the cold without so much as a good-bye. I hope she doesn't change her mind for a while.

I feel so much better about everything—I think we all do. Lillie, Jessie, and me had such a good visit at Lillie's cabin. She showed us a quilt she had made, calling it her memory quilt. We had never seen such a pretty quilt and told Lillie so. She fairly beamed at us then told us how it came to be. Each scrap, she said, had come from a part of her life, some parts good and some not so good. There was an embroidered handkerchief of her mama's, pieces of her pa's overcoat, scraps of an old linsey-woolsey dress her friend Ely had given her right after her pa had died when she was just a girl. Another scrap was from a dress that must've held a bad memory, for she passed right over it and didn't say where it was from. In the middle of all of these delicately sewed pieces was two appliquéd wildflowers, one yellow and one blue, for each of the dresses Jack had bought her when they first met.

"I was going to sell it in a church raffle back in Virginia City," Lillie told us, smiling softly, "a kind of send-off to my past . . . But then a preacher's wife came to look at it, and she said something that made me think I ought to keep it."

"What?" Jessie and me both said at the same time, and we looked at each other and grinned. Lillie smiled, too, then gazed down at her quilt.

"She told me that a good quilter doesn't choose the pieces with her eyes but with her heart. She said if you do that, then no matter how ugly it might seem at first, how bad the colors clash, the quilt would always turn out good in the end when you put the whole thing together." Lillie looked back up at us then. "Suddenly I didn't want to give my memories away. I wanted to keep them, because I knew I had chose the pieces with my heart."

"That's about the prettiest story I've ever heard," Jessie said softly, and I couldn't help but agree.

December 2, 1869 . . .

The "fickle lady" has decided to stay on another day.

I went to fetch some water from the spring this afternoon and found Stem and Rose sitting close on the bank of the stream as they tried their hands at fishing. I almost joined them when I heard Rose talking about how she hated "that Mr. Carey fellow through and through for hurting the horse and his own little boy." I stood back a ways then and watched Stem set his own pole down gently as he peered over at Rose, real thoughtfullike.

"Hate makes ye a black heart, and it don't change the other feller none either," he said, then cocked his head to one side. "That's lesson—what number be it, sis?" There was a pause as Rose cast her line in, then she nodded to herself.

"Eight hundred and ninety-nine," she announced gravely, and I couldn't help but smile to myself.

"Thet many, eh? Well, I ain't one to dispute sech a figger—not with a smart whip like you as my counter, but there's more to be had. If anything ever happened to me, I'd want to make sure ye'd be ready for the world."

"Ain't nothing ever gonna happen to you, Stem," Rose said, her voice so sure. "The preacher said God gives us whole new bodies, so I'm praying for you a new one. I thought about just praying for you a new leg, but I figured if you could get a whole body, you'd probably want that."

I saw Stem smile then, and he cleared his throat. "I thank ye for that, sis," Stem said. "I always figgered I'd have to wait to git the whole package once't I got t' the pearly gates."

"Well, you can't go to heaven just yet," Rose said matter-of-factly. "God's too smart for that, Stem. He knows we need you here."

"Well then, thet settles it, don't it, sis?" Stem chuckled and Rose giggled. I felt my heart swell with love for the dear old man who had loved all of us like we were his own.

I left them like that and came back to the cabin, thinking of how I might thank Stem without giving it away that I'd overheard their little talk. It wasn't until a few hours later, when Quinn and Jack said they were wanting to take a trip into town, knowing the good weather wouldn't last forever, that I found my chance.

I asked Stem if he was planning on going into town, too. He shook his old white head at me and grinned. "No, I promised Jessie I'd finish that quilt frame, and today I aim to do jes that," he said amiably. "Might as well jes leave the young'uns to me, too. The little britches ain't been too keen on me jes takin' Rose fishin'. If'n I git Jessie's quilt frame done, I might ought to take them all down to the crick for a day of it."

Stem was smiling with his head kind of cocked to one side like he always did, as if he was already imagining the afternoon, and before I knew it, I had leaned over, hugging him tight as I planted a kiss on his leathery old cheek.

"What's thet for?" he said, shocked, but I could see he was touched, too.

"Because as hard as I try, I can't find enough words for how I feel in my heart," I said then, feeling my eyes mist over.

"Well now, honey, ye don't hafta. I feel the same 'bout you, too." Stem grinned then and touched his hand to the cheek I had kissed, shaking his head. "Said it before, and I'll say it agin: If'n I was younger I would've give that Irish whelp a run for his money," he declared, and we both laughed.

December 3, 1869 . . .

The worst thing has happened. Oh, Lord, I would pray for courage to get through this, but I don't think even courage is enough to keep my heart from breaking to pieces.

We were coming home from town and had only pulled into the yard of the ranch when we heard the awfulest crying—heart-wrenching keening that I will never forget until the day I die. I ran through the door of the cabin to find Rose holding Patrick and John-Charles tight in her arms, rocking, the awful crying I'd heard coming from her. I asked her where Stem was, feeling an awful foreboding in my body, like my legs wanted to give out, like I didn't really want to hear. Then she told me, her voice shaking as Quinn held her and the boys. Bonny's husband had come back, had seen Midnight in the corral. Stem and the kids were in the house and hadn't heard him ride up. He'd slammed open the door and stood there looking at them with an angry smirk on his face. Then his eyes had fallen to their feet, and he saw the moccasins Bonny had made them.

"He took his gun out, Mama, started waving it at us," Rose sobbed. "Stem stepped in front of us and told him they'd step outside. I yelled at Mr. Carey not to hurt my uncle, and he just laughed and said I was blind. He said white girls couldn't have Negroes for uncles."

Rose was crying so hard the words poured out of her in a gush of sobs and hiccups. "Mr. Carey shoved Stem when he went through the door, and Stem shoved him back. Then Stem turned to me and said for me not to ever forget, said sometimes it's a good thing to be blind . . . Mr. Carey pushed his gun up against Stem's back and made him walk up the hill. You know Stem can't walk fast, but Mr. Carey kept pushing him with the gun. We couldn't see after that, but Mama, we heard a shot! Then Mr. Carey came back, and Stem wasn't with him. We wanted to hurry to find Stem and help him, but Mr. Carey told us to stay in the house and keep our mouths shut or we'd be even sorrier than we already were. Then he got back on his horse and rode off. Mama, you gotta find Stem and help him! I'm afraid Mr. Carey hurt him!"

"Which way did they go, lass?" I heard Quinn ask her gently, but I was already out the door, running past Jack and Lillie and Jessie, who had just pulled into the yard behind us in the other wagon. I ran blindly, but somehow I found Stem. He was lying just over the hill that sloped down to the stream. His clothes were still smoking from the gunshot when I got to him.

I knelt down, trying not to cry as I waved the smoke away from him so I could unbutton his vest, but he put his shaky hand on mine. "Don't," he rasped. "Too late."

"It don't seem right, someone so young'd have so much hate," Stem said then, almost like he was talking to himself. "Whenever I thought to hate, I'd jes look at this land God made—or some sweet child, like little Rose, with so much God in her new eyes—and I'd think, 'What's to hate?'"

My tears were falling on his face as he drew in a quick, sharp breath. "What's to hate?" he said again, a bare whisper, and I looked up and saw Jessie running toward us, her skirts flying. Quinn, Lillie, and Jack weren't far behind. The whole world was running, but none of us were quick enough.

"Lord Almighty, Callie," he whispered, "I wish this was a bad dream an' I could jes wake up."

I believe Stem did wake up . . . just not for us . . . not for us.

Stem died in my arms just as Jessie reached us, sobbing, "Not before me! Oh, Lord, don't take *him* before *me!*" She knelt down and touched his face, and he looked at her one last time with love, then regret. And then he closed his eyes, and there was a hush that seemed to still the air around us. When I looked down at Stem the regret was gone, and he looked younger somehow. There was a softness to his face I'd never seen and a smile that looked a bit like relief and joy mixed together.

It was like he was remembering . . . remembering how good it was to see God's face again . . .

I'm not sure how much later it was, but after we'd gotten Stem's body back to his and Jessie's cabin and were beginning the sad work of laying him out, I looked up to see Jack, Quinn, and Coy saddled up and riding out. I knew they were going after Stem's killer. All I can think of as I write this is, no matter what happens, it's not enough. It won't bring him back. It *won't* bring him back . . .

How long ago was it that you told me I'd get used to death, dear friend? After all these years that's passed, I still haven't, Stem. I guess it's like you always liked to say, this might be one trick even a young pup can't learn.

December 4, 1869 . . .

Early—They tracked Mr. Carey to one of the meadows in the high country. Quinn told me he was so busy looking over his shoulder, galloping his horse and shooting wild at them, that he failed to see the bluff ahead. His horse saw it, though, and all of a sudden it balked and reared, and Mr. Carey fell off. He was still holding the horse's reins, though, trying to get back on, but the horse was wild. And right on the edge of that bluff, the horse reared again, and Mr. Carey backed up to miss getting trampled— and slipped over the edge. They found him at the bottom with his neck broke and ended up burying him where he lay.

I don't know what to write, what to feel. God's justice? That's what Jack says. But I don't feel any sort of justice about it, and I won't pretend to know the Lord's mind. But I couldn't imagine Him feeling good about any of this, either.

Knowing Mr. Carey is dead doesn't bring Stem back to

us, and that's the *only* thing that would make me feel better right now.

I have just returned from helping Jessie get Stem's body ready for burying. We could hear Jack's awful hammering of the coffin as we worked at the grim task, and I looked up once to see Jessie staring at an object shadowed in the corner of their little cabin, a large wooden ring standing on two stout legs. "He finished my quilt frame, just like he promised," she said, her voice soft. When she dropped her head and looked at me her large dark eyes were so full of the hurt I felt, I wanted to run away.

"I went looking for Stem this mornin'," she said softly. "Sounds crazy, I know, but I kept thinkin' maybe somewhere outside he'd be able to come to me, tell me he was okay." She shook her head. "I kept walkin' and walkin', and I started thinkin', *Where is he that he can't tell me he's okay—and who is God not to let him?*" She was silent for a long while, then she looked at me, looked right in my eyes and said, "You think God only answers white folks' prayers, Callie?"

If I hadn't been sure my heart was already broke her words would have done it for sure . . . "He didn't answer about my baby sister, Rose, or my pa—or my ma before that," I said slowly. "I think He's color blind to us, Jessie, when He chooses to say yes—and when we don't want to hear His no."

"Jes seems like more no's than yes's, don't it?" Jessie said as I helped her dress Stem in his Sunday best, trying so hard not to cry that my hands trembled. Jessie looked down at him for a moment, then at me, studying my face for a long time. I don't know what she saw, but when she started talking, her eyes took on a faraway look.

"Yes, ma'am, I've been told no before . . . ," she said softly. "I asked the Lord, begged Him, not to let them sell my man and little ones away from me—but they was sold anyways. When I got my freedom, I asked Him to help me find my family. But I never found them, not a one, and oh, how I searched! It was in one of the last of those towns that I gave up on life. White man in town caught me by the sleeve and told me my free papers didn't mean nothin', said any of my kind would serve him as he pleased and if I felt to say anything, he'd just shoot me."

Jessie sighed and told me how she'd got away from that man, how she ran and ran until she got all the way out of town, how when night fell she found some thick brush to hide in. "I was sittin' in that brush when it struck me. I thought, *Oh, what's the use?* I remembered stories my own mama told me about the Lord comin' for folks on fiery chariots, and I looked up in the night sky and said, 'Why don't Ye jes come get me, then? There ain't nothin' good come of my life, and now I can't even find my family. So jes come get me. It don't even have to be a fiery chariot. Amen.'" Jessie turned to me then, smiling a wry smile.

"As ye can see, He didn't come. Well, I got to cryin' real pitiful-like when I saw He wasn't comin'. I was cryin' over all I'd lost, and suddenly this big voice comes up inside of me, getting so loud I felt it on the outside, too. Scared me something silly. The voice say, 'Jessie, yer not finished yet. Ye ain't lost yer family. This is just part of the journey ye gotta walk without 'em.' So I got up and started walkin' again.

"One night I set down to rest, and I was struck by how lonely I was, so I decided to try talkin' to the Lord again. I said, 'Lord, I've walked a goodly part of this journey now alone. I sure would appreciate some company.' Didn't think any more about it. I got up next mornin' same as always and started walkin' again. 'Bout noon was when I came across yer wagon train. Then Stem showed up on that horse of his'n, with that smile a mile wide, and I knew the Lord had sent him. But I tested the poor man all the way to California." Jessie chuckled with the memory, but then her smile dimmed, as if she suddenly remembered Stem was gone.

"I must be a fool," she said suddenly, startling me.

"Why would you say such a thing?"

"Because I fixed it my mind the Lord was done tryin' me," she said, frowning. "Ain't none of us gonna be done with trials 'til we die." She looked at me, her smile trembly. "I just didn't want to be alone in the trials no more, is all."

"But you aren't alone, Jessie," I said in a rush, trying not to cry. "You still have us."

"Yes I do, at that," she said, walking slowly over to the beautiful quilt that had been spread so proudly over the little bed in the corner. She pulled the quilt off and tucked it gently around Stem's still, cold form.

"It just doesn't seem right for ye to be so quiet, husband," she whispered.

When she looked at me again, she tried to smile, but

the smile seemed lost in the lines and wrinkles that were etched in her face like a living map of pain and endurance.

Later—Just woke up from a bad dream. I was holding Stem in my arms again, yelling up at the sky, *No, No, No!* over and over again . . .

Why is it that we yell *No*, knowing good and well how useless it is? Do we think if we yell loud enough that God will listen? Or is it so we can't hear the horrible sound of our own hearts breaking?

We'd laid Stem out on his and Jessie's kitchen table. The men had carried Jack and Lillie's table in, too, to support his cold, rigid form now covered with Jessie's beautiful quilt. Then, as night fell, we'd gathered around him to begin the long, sad vigil until dawn, huddling together like calves lost in a storm. Jack tried to lighten things. "Remember when Stem . . ." I can't *remember* now what he even said, but I remember we kind of laughed at first, then we all cried. Everyone of us.

Finally the men sent us women away, saying we should put the kids to bed and get some sleep ourselves. Sadly, Lillie and I hugged Jessie as she slipped into the bed she and Stem had shared, then we went to our own cabins, leading the weary youngsters along the dark paths.

I sent the kids to their beds and fell asleep almost immediately myself but awoke just as quickly when the dream stirred my thoughts. Quinn heard me crying out just as he'd stuck his head in the door to check on us. He settled beside me on the bed, trying to comfort me, wrapping his big arms around me, arms that had been there to hug me when I lost my pa and baby sister . . . when Jack rode away and I feared never seeing him again. All I could think was *Why?* I didn't even realize I'd said the word out loud until Quinn turned me to him.

"There are no reasons I can find fitting, lass," he said softly. "Never will be—none ever good enough, that is." I couldn't see his face, but I heard the horrible grief in his voice and the sigh that followed. "'Tis sure the devil's boots don't creak when he sneaks up on us," he whispered, and I knew by the tone he was thinking of his brother, the one we named Patrick after.

Suddenly I felt the need to have Rose and Patrick with us. I scooped Patrick out of his bed and put his sleepy body in between Quinn and me, then I went for Rose, too, but she refused to be comforted. "Go away, Mama," she said, turning her back to me, giving the wall her grief instead of me as she sobbed quietly in the dark.

I thought to go back to bed, but instead I lit the lamp and settled at the kitchen table so I could write this, hoping I might feel better if I got the feelings out of me and onto paper, but I don't.

I feel like Elisha tonight, running from the evil that's at my heels, like I'm just running and running to that desert place—only it's in my mind that I'm running. I have to wonder, If I was running for real, would I come back . . . ?

Oh, Lord, sometimes I just want to climb out of my skin, just shake it off like a dirty overcoat. Just climb out and call to You, Lord, like Jessie did, to come get me, come take me away from all this ugliness I've seen.

Where's your faith? *a small voice whispers, and I say,* It's here. See, I know that You are here, God, I know You are creator of all. I know You're a God of love that's so pure, like when I looked at Stem, dying, and saw him looking back at me—that love, that's You . . . It's just that sometimes this world dirties that love, and it's so hurtful to witness . . .

December 5, 1869 . . .

The sun is dawning over the mountains in the distance, and I feel like it has no right.

I slept no more last night. Occasionally, looking out our cabin's window, I could see the glow of a cheroot in the dark outside Jessie's porch, and I knew it was Jack's. When it got light enough for me to see him, I watched him walk slowly to the barn. Through the open doors I saw him bend beside the coffin he'd built and lift it onto his shoulder. He looked up and spotted me watching him through the window then, his eyes so full of sorrow. He carried the coffin into Jessie's cabin then emerged again and trudged slowly my way. I opened the door and motioned toward the coffee I'd poured for him at the table.

"Seems like no matter where we go, sis, we always end up makin' a trip to the grave," he said softly, and I felt the tears start fresh tracks down my cheeks. Tears for Stem, tears for us.

"It's been too many trips, Jack," was all I could manage to say, and he just nodded and headed back down the path to Jessie's cabin.

I went to the spring to fetch some water, and when I came back, Patrick was already up and about. As I opened the door, he looked startled, then said, "Shut the door, Mama. It's . . . it's cold out there!" Then he burst into tears.

We buried Stem just before sunset, and if there were any days I could erase from my mind, it would be this one. It hurts to write about this, but it hurts more not to. I'm not sure if that would make any sense to anyone but me.

I know it was cold, but I can't remember *being* cold. I remember Patrick holding my hand so tight as he squared his little shoulders, trying so hard to be strong for me like his pa. Willa kept taking a few steps forward, then she'd stand still for a moment, only to take another few steps, like she wasn't sure where to stand. Bonny wept softly as her little ones clutched her skirts. Her beautiful hair, cut off to show her mourning—not for her husband, Coy told me earlier, but for Stem.

"She's no hypocrite. I'll give her that," Quinn said under his breath as he stood by my side. When I looked at her, I saw her eyes catch mine and tried to smile, but I couldn't seem to get it right. Jessie saw me struggling, and she started crying, then I did, too.

Then I wondered whether people knew if they were going out of their minds. If they did, I hoped I would, so I could pretend I wasn't there.

Jack shifted then, standing on the other side of me beside the grave—as he had done twice before. But this time he didn't run. He remained, firm and unmoving, with Lillie on the other side of him holding John-Charles's hand. I couldn't help thinking that Jack was like those wild mustangs, so determined to keep the ground they had found—no matter what. He cleared his throat, but a sob escaped anyway as he opened the family Bible.

I felt Quinn's arm go around my shoulders as Jack began to read the Scripture verse—but I don't recall which one. Then I heard him say good-bye to Stem, heard everyone saying good-bye but me, and I looked away, trying to escape it . . . My eyes rested on Willa, who had been standing silent through the whole thing, her gaze fixed on that freshly turned mound of dirt.

"I guess no one knows he came and helped me from time to time. No, he wouldn't have told it," she said to no one in particular, shaking her head.

"He was too good for this world," she blurted out suddenly, almost angry, surprising us all. Then she burst into tears and fairly ran for her wagon. We all stood there, just watching her go, too weary to do anything about it.

The men began to lower the coffin, and I saw Jessie take a sudden step forward. She was looking down into the hole, and suddenly I knew what she was thinking.

"Jessie," I said softly, and she hesitated, looking at me.

"No, yer right, Callie," she said, almost a whisper. "I don't have to climb in there to feel dead, do I?"

Quinn, Jack, and Coy hurried to cover the grave after that, worried that Jessie might try something if they didn't. But I could see that she was played out. Lillie and I went over and stood by her side as they finished up. Even after Coy and Bonny left, we stayed with her.

"I just can't leave yet," she told us more than once, so the men took Patrick and John-Charles back to the cabin, and Lillie and me stayed, wrapping ourselves with the blankets they brought out. Then they brought us coffee, and we still stayed with Jessie, watching as the little light that was left dipped down behind the mountains.

Jack finally came and fetched Lillie, saying it wasn't good for her or the baby to be out in the cold. He handed me the Bible as he left. Then Quinn was walking toward us, carrying something in his arms. In that quiet way of his, he showed us the good-sized stone he'd carved Stem's name in, just like he'd done on that rock in Nebraska for Pa. He couldn't fit much else, so underneath Stem's name, he simply put "John 15:13."

I held the lantern up and read the scripture out loud to Jessie. "Greater love hath no man than this, that a man lay down his life for his friends" is what it said.

We watched Quinn dig another, smaller hole and settle the stone in it at the head of the grave. "It's fitting, isn't it?" I said gently, and I saw Quinn turn and look up at Jessie, hoping he had done something to help somehow. Her eyes met his with such gratefulness—and such heartache.

"More than fittin'," she said softly.

I felt something wet hit my face and looked up to the sky to see the first thick flakes of snow falling hard and heavy, spiraling down toward us through the sky, and for some strange reason, I couldn't help hoping it never stopped.

Later—Still snowing.

I just came down from trying to comfort Rose, but she's having none of it. I don't understand it, but I can't shake the feeling she's blaming herself in some odd way . . .

Quinn told me that he heard Rose crying softly from her little loft room while I was with Jessie. He said he climbed up to comfort her but found Patrick leaning over her bed, patting her back softly with his chubby little hand, saying, "Don't cry, sister, don't cry." He said he noticed John-Charles on the other side of the bed then, watching intently for a moment before taking his side of Rose's back and beginning to pat her, too.

Quinn crept back down the ladder before any of them noticed he was there.

"'Twas a sacred moment," he said with tears in his eyes. "One I won't forget as long as I live. If you could have seen them comforting her . . ."

"I just can't understand why she wouldn't come to his grave with us," I said, tears in my own eyes. "She loved him as much as any of us, maybe more."

"You've just answered it yourself, lass," Quinn said then. "'Tis said that the chief mourner is rarely found at the funeral. Our Rose, her feelings have always run deep. So deep it worries me sometimes. I fear one day they could lead her wrong."

"She wasn't wrong to love Stem," I said, looking up into his worried eyes, and I saw a gentling come in them.

"No," he said softly. "If loving such a man as him were wrong, we'd all be at fault, wouldn't we?"

He hugged me to him then, and as he did, I silently prayed that God would see Rose through this terrible time—see us all through.

He is our only hope. I know *none* of us have the strength ourselves.

December 8, 1869 . . .

Cold wind today. I keep wishing I could tell Stem just one more thing. What would it be? My mind races, I think of so much: *I love you. I miss you, miss your laughter and your love . . .* I suppose I could write things forever, so maybe I don't wish I could tell him one more thing, I just wish he was here. I know we're not supposed to question God, but I can't help it. Can't help wondering why. My faith feels so shaky . . .

Rose finally came down from the loft this evening after everyone else had turned in. I was sitting up by myself, mending Quinn's trousers, when I heard her step quietly down the ladder and pad her way over to the rocker where I sat sewing. She stood, watching me in silence for a bit, then stepped in front of me. I set my sewing aside, and she came to me, curling up in my lap just as she always did when troubled.

I told her I'd tried to run from pain, too, tried to hide, but I'd found out hiding was lonely.

"It's my fault, Mama," she blurted out, and then it was as if a dam had broke open and she started to cry. "It's all my fault. I prayed for Stem to have a new body—but I didn't mean for God to take him to heaven." She sobbed harder, and I hugged her to me, whispering comfort in her ear the best I could, feeling tears of my own trickle down my face. "It's not your fault, honey," I whispered. "God just chose to take him home."

"But I thought *this* was his home," Rose said, the misery of trying to understand so strong in her blue eyes. Then her eyes turned angry.

"I hate Mr. Carey," she said then. "And I don't care if I have a black heart for it, either. Stem, Jessie, and Coy are *all* black, and I'm gonna be just like them!" She burst into a fresh round of tears then, leaning against me, saying, "Why, oh why, Mama?" until I felt another rip in my heart, wondering just how much a heart *could* take.

I didn't try to tell her the whys of it, for I didn't know myself. But I kept her hugged close to me, and we rocked for a long while like that, not just mother and daughter, I thought, but two hurt souls, trying to find comfort the best way we knew how . . .

He will swallow up death in victory; and the Lord GOD will wipe away tears from off all faces. . . .
—ISAIAH 25:8

December 9, 1869 . . .

I wish I could describe how I feel. Sometimes there just isn't the words . . .

I look at the words I've just written, and they are nothing—mean nothing. Just dark scratches on a page.

Please help me, Lord.

December 11, 1869 . . .

I saw the preacher pull into our yard just as I was coming from the spring this morning, my hands almost froze to the pails as I walked slowly up the hill toward him. I saw Preacher look toward the corrals where the men were, then to me, and he smiled a sad kind of smile and headed in my direction. He took the pails from me like he needed to busy himself as he talked. He said he'd heard about Stem as soon as he rolled back into town and it hit him nearly as hard as the deaths of his own parents. He shook his head, like he was trying to understand, then looked sideways at me.

"There was something about him," he said softly. "Something I saw that first night, like he was there to comfort me—not the other way around."

I felt my eyes burn a bit, nodding. "Stem was always a rock to all of us," I said. "I don't know what we'll do without him—what Jessie will do without him . . ."

He looked down at me then, his dark eyes so full of sorrow and compassion that I felt I could look into them forever. "Trials come to test our faith," he said, setting the pails down, and he turned and looked toward the mountains that loomed in the distance. "Beautiful country," he said, and I laughed kind of a harsh laugh that surprised even me.

"We thought it was going to be our promiseland here," I said. "And Stem believed it more than anyone."

Preacher looked at me thoughtfully, then said, "Sometimes I think of all those poor souls Moses led out of Egypt. They saw the Red Sea part, ate bread from heaven, and still, when the trials came, they forgot. They ended up wandering year after year because they forgot God was God . . . They forgot that all they had to do was step forward and reach their hands out and God would've led them home. Don't let death take your hope from you, Mrs. McGregor," he said, turning toward the path that led to Jessie's cabin. Then he stopped for a moment, looking across the land again, and he turned back to look at me one last time. "This *is* your promiseland. Stem wouldn't have wanted you to forget."

I stood outside a long time after dinner, just as the sun was starting to dip behind the mountains, and I felt my eyes drawn to the sky . . . so much sky. As I looked up into that ocean of blue, I couldn't help thinking on what Preacher had said. *Stem wouldn't have wanted you to forget.* The words whispered to me again, and as I lifted my arm up and held my hand to the sky, watching the fading sunlight filter through my fingers, a peace came over me that I had never felt before, warm and comforting. I shut my eyes and prayed then. "Don't let us forget, Lord," I whispered, and I could've sworn I felt the firm grasp of a hand covering my own . . .

Rose asked if she could go down and see Jessie tonight. I had so many chores to catch up on, but it was the first time since Stem died that she had mentioned going anywhere outside the house, so we went, trudging through the fresh snow, Jasper and Honey tagging along, strangely silent and nuzzling Rose's hand as if they understood.

As Jessie opened the door to us, we stepped into the warm little cabin, and I saw Rose's eyes go to the spot where Stem always sat to play his fiddle. The fiddle was still there, gleaming by the light of the fire, and I saw her face start to crumple as she looked Jessie in the eye for the first time.

"I'm so sorry, Jessie," Rose sobbed, great tears streaming

down her face, her little shoulders shaking. She told Jessie about her prayer then, and I saw Jessie smile, but it was a grim kind of smile.

"There, there, sis," Jessie said, her large, callused hand patting the small of Rose's back. "Ain't no one's fault. The Lord jes allowed this to be Stem's time, is all. Preacher said there ain't nothin' the Lord don't know. We jes got to trust He knows best." I saw Jessie's eyes go distant then, to that place we go when we give up looking for the answers the world gives us. The look was sad and questioning, then finally accepting.

Rose wasn't so accepting. "Well, if I was God, I'd know it wasn't best to take Stem from us," she said hotly, and it was on the tip of my tongue to correct her when I saw the barest hint of a smile cross Jessie's face.

"Well, ye ain't God, child, so don't go talkin' like that," she said sternly but gently, like she understood. Rose looked up at her, sensing that, then placed her hand in Jessie's. She looked around the little cabin with a kind of longing.

"Can I stay the night with you, Jessie?" she asked suddenly, and when Jessie's eyes met mine we both knew without saying she was trying to get as near to feeling Stem as she could. Because Jessie understood that, she agreed.

"Can't think of any way better to spend my evenin'," Jessie said.

When I left them, they had their heads bent over a small, leather-bound box that Stem had carried everywhere he went. As I trudged back up to our cabin, Jasper and Honey in tow, I remembered something Stem said long ago. "Sometimes the reasons fer things happenin' don't seem good," he'd told me, "but the Almighty has a way of makin' good of it all in the end."

December 13, 1869 . . .

It's a mystery to me why things panned out like they did tonight. My reasons for going out to Willa's place were purely selfish, but I think the good Lord had other plans . . .

I'd told Quinn when he hitched the team for us that the trip was for Rose, but I think it was for me, too. No sooner had I bundled the two little ones in the back of the wagon and hawed the team away from the ranch than this strange, childish thought came to me: *If you don't see it, it isn't real.* I thought I could almost pretend Stem's death hadn't really happened. In spite of my praying, the look of Rose's forlorn little face looking up to the sky from time to time throughout the day had got me down, and all I could think of was to get away from it all. By the time we reached Willa's place, I started pondering why I'd felt so drawn to come when I hardly knew her at all. I saw Coy's rig and knew he would be visiting with Bonny. Life went on, I thought, whether we felt like it should or not. I considered leaving, but then I spotted Willa standing on her porch, like she was expecting us.

She watched me help Rose down and gather Patrick into my arms, then she said, "Seems like everyone had the same idea today." Without another word, she reached to take Patrick from me. He looked at her, wide-eyed, then something in his face showed he liked what he saw, and he went to her. Willa acted like it was nothing, but I could see it touched her as she led me and Rose into the house wordlessly.

The kitchen was filled with the smell of fresh coffee and fresh-baked bread. It was decorated pretty, too, with little engravings and dry flowers on the wall and a floor so clean you could eat off it. As I sat down at the table with Willa, I couldn't help thinking everything seemed made for company, like the house had just been waiting. Willa poured us each a cup of coffee, and not long after Rose and Patrick had scampered off to find Bonny's little ones, we started talking—or I should say I did. I told Willa about Stem's headstone, and about Rose, then I told her about the preacher coming and what he'd said. Willa nodded through most of it until I came to the part about the preacher. Her eyes fairly sparked with fire then.

"Well, that's fine to *say*," she said. "But where's the proof of it? Seeing is believing, I always say. And I haven't seen much proof in my life . . ." I saw the spark in her eyes dwindle a bit, and she looked down at the gold ring she wore, rubbing it softly with her finger. The prongs where the stone should've been were smoothed over by wear, and I wondered how many times she had rubbed her finger over that ring.

"I used to believe in a lot of things, Callie," she said, not looking up at me. "The reason I wear this ring is to remind me why I don't believe anymore." She told me then about the girl she was before the war, about the handsome young boy she used to race every day after school until she realized one day she *wanted* him to catch her. How he'd become a soldier for the North and how her mama had given her the ring when they announced their engagement.

"Have you ever looked in someone's eyes and it's like you

know him and he *knows* you and you don't even need words because you feel like you've come home somehow?" Willa looked at me, and I nodded, thinking of Quinn, realizing all I had as her lonely eyes turned to look out her window.

"Shawn's grandmother lived in Kentucky and had written to him of a beautiful diamond that had been passed down from generation to generation—that he should have it to give to me. She was afraid to mail it, with the war and all, so he decided he would ride to her house when he was given his next leave." Willa smiled, but her smile was sad. "I was so afraid for him that I tried to convince him to go west with me, but he wouldn't. He had given his word, he said, so he would stand and fight. He was like a great lion of a young man, big and strong, and I always imagined he had to be made big to hold such a heart as his . . ."

Willa looked up at me, and I saw the tears in her eyes even as she tried to blink them away. "He said he would come back—but he never did. I prayed and prayed, but he never came back. So I quit praying . . ."

She sighed, then she glanced over at the little table under the window and said, "There are my advice-givers, now." She pointed to an old silver-edged double frame propped up on the table holding a picture of a distinguished-looking man on the left and a petite, smiling woman on the right. The woman looked so much like Willa I knew the people in the pictures had to be her parents.

"I talk, and they listen," she said matter-of-factly, and she smiled wryly. "I suppose I shouldn't complain about the arrangement—at least I never have to worry about disagreements."

"It sounds lonely to me," I said softly, feeling my heart

go out to her, having just two old photographs to keep her company. Willa shrugged, like she was trying to shrug off my sympathy, too.

"It's better than nothing," she said, trying to sound casual. Suddenly I felt a surge of love well up in me for her that I didn't know I had. It was like I could see her as she truly was, lonely and hurt and trying to find her way . . . and I thought, even as hurt as I was, and as much as I'd been through, how lost I'd be without God.

"God is real, Willa," I said, feeling my own faith start to lift a bit as I spoke—like I was talking to me as well as her. "He answers us. It's just sometimes the answers aren't what we expect."

Willa didn't look at me but picked up the coffeepot and poured another cup for each of us. I might have thought she wasn't even listening if I hadn't seen her hand shaking a bit as she poured.

"I don't know how you can talk so sure after what happened to Stem. God is good, they say. What's good about that?" she said, then raised her chin a bit, defiant. "Like I said before, seeing is believing, and I haven't seen anything good yet."

I'd started to tell her sometimes we can't see His reasons, right off, but just as I did, Coy and Bonny and the kids came tumbling into the kitchen to tell us it had started snowing again, and since I didn't have runners on the wagon, Coy thought it best for me to head home. I hugged Willa and Bonny and her kids and made my way out to the wagon, and as I turned the team to head home, I glanced at Willa and was shocked by the longing I saw in her eyes as she stared after us. Like her eyes wanted what her mouth couldn't yet admit . . .

Her look kept with me as I pushed my team into a fast clip through the icy wind and large flakes of snow that had already blanketed the ground in white. The look made me think of something my mama had told me long ago when we had been so worried about Jack: *"Doesn't matter how much a person denies believing in God or Jesus,"* she'd said. *"They believe, all right. We were all born believing. All you have to do is look in their eyes, and you'll see the truth of it."*

I had seen the truth of it in Willa's eyes tonight. I just wish I knew how to help her heart. And why does this have to happen now? Why, when I'm fighting to understand things myself?

Lord, there's so much I don't understand . . .

Will I ever?

December 14, 1869 . . .

Lillie's condition left her feeling poorly today, so Jessie and I decided to lend a hand, making sure a good fire was stoked and filling the copper tub on her stove with plenty of water to last the day before we got to our own chores. As we walked back from the stream a second time, I told Jessie about me and Willa's talk, how I went out there to "hide from it all" and ended up hearing myself telling Willa to have faith in spite of my own faith feeling so shaky.

"Funny thing is," I told Jessie, "I *did* feel a bit stronger after we talked."

Jessie nodded. "Sometimes I think the Lord gives us others to think on so we can't think on ourselves so much," she said. "Did me good havin' Rose come spend the night. Just before you two came, I was lying in bed, fixing to cry myself silly when the Lord spoke to me. He say, 'Jessie, I ain't give up on you, so you don't give up on Me.'" Jessie looked over at me. "I say right back, 'I'm just sad, Lord—but I ain't gave up on You.' Then I say louder, so the ol' devil can hear, 'I ain't gave up!'"

Jessie shook her head a bit. "Next thing I know, I'm lying next to Rose, pattin' her little back in the dark 'til she falls asleep, and I say, 'Well, Ye made sure I couldn't give up, didn't Ye, Lord?'"

We smiled a bit at each other, then Jessie said, "Good Lord sure don't let us stay quitters long." I saw her look at the cabins, her eyes trailing over the land, and it struck me that out of all of us, Jessie had the hardest road to walk. But she'd kept on walking. She turned back to me then, studying me with those large, soulful brown eyes of hers, and in them I saw a lot of tragedy, a little triumph, but most of all, I saw the will to survive.

"How did you ever get so strong?" I asked then, and she looked at me curiously.

"Why, I ain't strong, Callie," she said matter-of-factly. "The Lord's strong for me. He know. Get as old as I am, ye get used to losin' a lot of things in yer life. But I lose my faith, I lose *me*."

I couldn't help thinking, as I watched Jessie working by my side until nearly dusk, how much like old Joshua she was, fighting the giants of her life, pressing on with that enduring faith of hers . . . as if her spirit senses what's over the hill even if her body doesn't . . .

Cold and windy tonight. There's just a dusting of new snow that came this evening—but enough to make the cattle work for their food. Quinn heads out for more wood as I write this. I told him to make sure Jessie is well stocked, too. She's a mighty woman of faith, but that takes a mighty heart, too . . . I pray the Lord will be with her tonight and comfort her in His arms.

I'm more tired than usual. I wish I could wake up and have it be spring already.

December 15, 1869 . . .

More snow. Quinn and Jack told me it's only the beginning of our winter as they headed for the barn this morning.

Rose, Patrick, and John-Charles are lying on the hill making snow angels.

I'm worried about our supplies getting low.

Later—We had no more than laid our heads down tonight when Jack came barreling into our cabin, Jessie already in tow, his voice hoarse and shaky, telling us Lillie was fixing to have the baby. I was up and dressed in no time. Jack grabbed my hand tight as we stepped into the deep snow, and it scared me in a way, for he hadn't held my hand like that since we were kids, when we lost our mama. The awful words, *It's too early, it's too early,* kept running over and over in my head as Jessie and I stumbled through the drifts in our skirts behind him. I felt Jack squeeze my hand once, like to remind himself I was still there. It wasn't until we got to the door of their cabin that he seemed to realize he was holding my hand like that. "The snow . . . ," he said, as if to explain, but I knew it was more than the snow.

Lillie tried to put on a brave face as we looked her over. Jack paced back and forth across the room until Jessie finally ordered him and a frazzled John-Charles down to our cabin. As Lillie watched the door shut, the tears she had been holding back filled her eyes.

"I should've listened to Jack," she said, her voice shaky. "He told me over and over to take it easy. It's all my fault if anything happens to our baby . . ."

"This baby's just decided to meet ye sooner than ye thought. Jes wantin' its own way, is all," Jessie said, patting Lillie's hand gently. "Now, that shouldn't surprise ye, honey, knowin' how Jack's always fixed on doin' things *his* own way . . ."

Lillie smiled a trembly smile, and Jessie and I did our best to comfort her when the pains came.

Their baby girl was born less than an hour later. So tiny . . . just a little slip of a thing. She hardly cried at all, and when she finally did cry, it was so soft, I felt like she was just a whisper away from leaving us. Lillie felt it, too, for she kissed the tiny cheek as tears coursed down her face. "Don't leave me," she whispered, trying to smile. "We've only just met."

I felt as if whatever was left of my heart was going to shatter into little pieces. I looked over at Jessie, who stayed quiet as she tidied up the room. But the sorrowful look in her eyes said it all.

Jack came in soon after, so I waited until we left the cabin to talk, to ask Jessie what she thought the little one's chances were. "That child don't need *chance*. She needs the good Lord to deliver her," she said. "He did good by Moses and Daniel, as I recollect. I figure He'll do the same for her." I saw Jessie's chin go out like it always did when she set her mind on something. "All we gots to have is faith."

I watched Jessie tromp with purpose through the drifts of snow down to the empty little cabin that had once been filled with fiddle music and laughter, and I couldn't help thinking I'd never seen someone so selfless, so willing to give in spite of all that had been taken from her. So determined to believe . . .

I wish I could be as determined. This last trouble is like a ruthless thief, coming back to steal the last of our resolve . . .

December 18, 1869 . . .

Cold, cloudy day. So quiet around here. The snow just keeps piling up, leaving us no chance of finding the doctor now . . . We were amazed when Willa came riding through the snow. She offered to help however she could, but Jack ended up asking us all to leave, saying he and Lillie just needed some time alone—that the quiet might help the baby nurse better.

But his words held more hope than his eyes. He stood there in the door of their cabin, looking so hurt, so lost, that I wanted to put my arms around him. He must have sensed it, too, because he held a hand up to me, like he didn't want me to come any closer. Or maybe he was just afraid of what I might say.

"He can't take her, sis," he said. "He just can't take her, too." It was the way he said it—like he was talking to someone else, like he was begging as he looked up to the cold night sky.

And I just knew it was God he was talking to.

Later—And a little child shall lead them . . .

I'm reminded of those words tonight as it was Rose who brought me our family Bible to read, looking so solemn as she sat down at my feet with Patrick and John-Charles planted on each side of her. I had thought to turn to Daniel, for we were almost to the story of the fiery furnace, but was surprised when I went to open it and it fell open to a page with a *another* little dried flower tucked in the crease that I never recalled seeing before. There was scripture under-lined, too: "My grace is sufficient for thee: for my strength is made perfect in weakness," it said. My eye caught some writing off to one side, and I was shocked to see it was Pa's spiky handwriting, not Mama's. Pa had wrote: "I am weak, Lord. Be strong in me for my family, for those I love."

No sooner had I read it out loud to Quinn and the children, I felt in my heart it was meant for Jack to hear. I tucked the Bible under my arm and trudged out in the snow to Jack and Lillie's cabin. Jack looked haggard when he answered my knock and let me in then went right back to the little stool he sat on next to Lillie's bed, his shoulders hunched over like he was carrying the weight of the world on them. Lillie looked up at me then, and I saw she had been crying.

"Jessie was just here," she said, then lowered her voice to a whisper of awful hopelessness. "She won't nurse, Callie. It's like she doesn't have the strength."

Can a heart die a thousand times? I didn't know what to say, so with trembling hands, I opened up the Bible, telling them what I'd found, and as I read the scripture, read Pa's words, I saw Jack's head raise up a bit.

"I wonder when Pa wrote that," Jack said, never taking his eyes off Lillie or their baby, but I saw something new pass between them then, like a spark of a memory. Then we prayed, all of us holding hands around the bed, trying to drown out the baby's silence with our pleas.

As I turned to leave, I saw the look on Jack's face had changed, Lillie's too, like they were willing to hope again. Jack stood like he wanted to say something, the Bible hanging from his hand as he just stared. I saw the tumble of emotions cross his handsome face, and I realized what he was trying to say. We weren't brother and sister for nothing.

"I love you, too, Jack," I said, and he smiled a relieved kind of smile before I shut the door behind me.

There is something I have never written about. It happened long, long ago, but sometimes it feels like it was only yesterday when the memory of it comes to me like a sharp, bittersweet pain that washes over my eyes and I see the baby twins that were only allowed to lie in my arms for just a few short days. I remember the agony of Quinn and me having to bury them with no minister, no comfort from any family but each other . . . and Rose asking questions and being too young to understand . . . It's a pain I wouldn't wish on my worst enemy and cannot bear for my brother.

There is a part of me that worries that Jack's faith—that all of our faith—can't hold up under this flood, Lord, that we've tread this water 'til we're so weary that all we can think to do is give up . . . Yet there's another part of me that's afraid to let go of Your hand, that deep down knows You will be the One to pull us out if we can just hang on . . .

December 23, 1869 . . .

I just haven't had the heart to write lately. Each day seems such a struggle, like walking through molasses. The weather is so bitter, yet we trudge out and make our way down to Jack and Lillie's cabin, we breathe our relief and thanks that the sweet baby has made it through another day. Then we pray.

Oh, how we pray.

December 24, 1869 . . .
Christmas Eve

I admit my heart was not in the celebrating mood when I woke this morning, but so much has changed . . .

It was Quinn's gentle nudge that got me up and going, saying how the children needed it—and we did, too—whether I thought so or not. Quinn bundled up, going to pick a tree with Rose, Patrick, and John-Charles, and I had set to cooking when I realized I needed water. Dutifully I pulled on the old wool overcoat and boots and trudged out the door.

I didn't seem to even notice the cold, my heart was so heavy as I walked to the spring, thinking on the baby, wondering how much of a chance something so small could have. I can't say how long I stood there, just thinking, when suddenly I heard the wild horses, the sounds of their pounding hooves and snorts startling me as I glanced down the canyon. I saw the herd was turning toward the stream, puffs of steam trailing up from their noses in the cold air.

I scrambled up onto an outcropping of rock to look as they trotted along a trail in the canyon below, and for a moment, the world was just me and those wild horses, and I felt my breath catch in my chest. There was such a beauty in that small moment, so much that it almost hurt, like being given a gift you weren't expecting.

Oh, how I wish I could describe the feelings that welled up in my chest, watching the sun glinting off their shiny coats, hearing their whinnies filling the air, blotting out the bad of the world and making me think good could come again. For just that moment, there were no worries or tears or darkness, just beauty, and it awed me to think how big God truly is. I realized what I was seeing was just a small part of His making, like looking at a few stitches on a big quilt. Then the thought struck me how sad He must be that we forget how big He really is . . .

I bowed my head right there on that hill and prayed for Lillie's baby. But my prayer was different than the others I had cried or stumbled through the past several days. *Giving this baby a chance at life is a small thing for You, Lord, so I won't doubt anymore that it can be done . . .*

After a while, the horses turned and made their way into the distance again, and I climbed down the hill, filled the water pails, and headed back toward the cabins. It wasn't until I came over the last rise that I saw Quinn coming for me at a quick pace.

"Gotta get back to your brother's cabin, lass. There's something you should be seein'," he said, all out of breath. Then he took the pails from me like they were nothing, and we fairly ran the rest of the way.

It wasn't until I got into the cabin, my heart beating out of my chest, that I realized something had changed. The heavy feeling of sorrow was gone, and I saw Jessie standing to one side, a real fine smile on her face for the first time since Stem died. Lillie grinned at me big and motioned for me to come over to the bed, and as I looked down at the baby, tears began to spill down my cheeks. The baby's fine, petal-like skin had pinkened, and she was nursing hungrily like I had never seen a baby nurse.

"I opened that Bible of your mama's this morning, Callie, and right in front of my eyes was the prayer I knew I was supposed to pray," Lillie said with big tears in her eyes. She laughed a little, too, then looked over at Jack, who was standing in the corner, holding John-Charles with a sheepish look on his face. "When I told Jack I thought we were supposed to pray it for the baby, he said, 'Well then, let's say it out loud so the good Lord will be sure to hear us.'"

Lillie scooted the Bible to herself with one hand, her voice taking on a soft note. "'Unto thee lift I up mine eyes, O thou that dwellest in the heavens,'" she read. "'As the eyes of servants look unto the hand of their masters, and as the eyes of a maiden unto the hand of her mistress; so our eyes wait upon the LORD our God, until that he have mercy on us. Have mercy upon us, O LORD, have mercy upon us . . .'"

"The doctor showed up right after that," Jack said then, with a kind of wonder on his face, and pointed in the direction of their little kitchen area where for the first time I noticed a stranger standing, warming his hands at their fireplace. The stranger turned to me and smiled like he knew me, and I felt a tiny shiver go up my back.

"I opened the door when I heard the knock, and he just walked right past me to the baby, took her out of Lillie's hands, and started looking her over with his back to us," Jack went on, still looking shocked. "Then he handed her back to Lillie, and she was all pink and crying—and not sick crying like before, but like she was hungry." Jack looked at the man, his eyes misting. "I don't know what you did, mister, but you saved my little girl, and I can't thank you enough for that."

"Well, now," the stranger said, his deep voice so humble. "The Lord always makes a way when there seems to be no way, doesn't He?"

We all stood there, motionless, for a bit, the silence so peaceful and heavy that we all jumped a little when the baby up and cried. Then we laughed, looking at each other with such joy as she took to her mother's breast again with such gusto.

"We named her Mercy," Lillie said, looking down at her daughter with love, "because that's what God gave us, Mercy."

"Can't think of a better name for a Wade to have, can you, sis?" Jack asked, and we all laughed again—even the doctor, who seemed to take as keen a liking to us as we did to him. He even helped Quinn get the tree set up in our cabin while I finished up dinner and carried it down to

Jack and Lillie's cabin. Even Jessie laughed a time or two, then we noticed it was snowing again, and the doctor said he had to go.

Jessie helped him on with his coat and then surprised even herself by hugging him. "I'm jes so grateful to ye for helpin' like ye did," she said, wiping her eyes. "I just thank the Lord for ye, sir."

The stranger had his hand on the door by then, but stopped and looked at Jessie for a long moment, then he smiled. "Blessed are those that mourn, for they shall be comforted," he said like a whisper, then he was gone.

"We didn't even get to ask his name," Jack said, looking over at Quinn. They both headed out the door to catch the doctor, only to return a short bit later. Willa was with them, coming to tell us the news of a Christmas service that was going to be held in town, but the doctor had up and disappeared. "No tracks or anything," Quinn said. "The snow is over two feet deep. How can there be no tracks?"

"Well, it wasn't Doc Eddy. Percy told me he took off for Deer Lodge over a week ago," Willa said, looking around our stunned little group. After we told her all that had happened, she crossed the room quickly and peered down at Mercy, who was now sleeping peacefully in her mother's arms.

"Well, I'll be. Mercy Wade," she said, swiping at her eyes, "you just might be the one to make me think there really is a God after all."

As one soul leaves the earth, so another comes into it . . .
I keep thinking of that saying. I know it may sound
strange, but somehow, I think little Mercy and Stem's souls
must have brushed past each other, that somehow an old
fellow in buckskins was able to add his prayer to ours.
"Ain't never left you in a lurch yet, Callie," I can just hear
him laugh. Quinn thinks that doctor was an angel sent by
God, and as crazy as it might sound to outsiders . . . well, if
they were here, if they saw what we saw, they would understand there's really no other answer but that.

When I held Mercy in my arms late tonight, those eyes
that looked up at me seemed so wise for such a tiny, elflike
creature . . . as if she's already seen the best of us all and
isn't so worried about tomorrows. I said a little prayer for
her then, and when I bent down and kissed her tiny cheek,
I whispered, "Fight, little one. Fight for all you're worth."
And I got the eeriest feeling as she stared up at me with
those eyes of hers that seemed to speak to me like a gentle
rebuke from heaven itself: *"It's you I'll be teaching how to
fight."*

Later—"Mama," Rose whispered, looking up at me so pen-
sively as I tucked her into bed. "Is the baby gonna live?"
When I told her yes, she hesitated and drew her doll close
to her. "Is it a boy or girl?"

"A girl," I said, and I told her how Uncle Jack and Aunt
Lillie had named her Mercy, for the mercy God had given
them.

Rose let out the breath she had been holding in, like

she had been carrying the weight of the world on those tiny shoulders of hers. "Then God gave me mercy, too," she said solemnly. "When I was praying, I told Him I understood he needed Stem, so maybe He could understand how I needed a girl in this family. I said I'd sure like a girl for Christmas, for if it was another boy, I felt I was done for."

"Aw, Rose," Patrick said sleepily from under his mountain of covers.

"Well, you're not done for, are you?" I said, feeling myself start to grin. As I climbed slowly down the ladder, I could hear Quinn's soft chuckle, and I saw him sitting in that big old rocking chair before the fire. I walked over to him, and he pulled me down on his lap, hugging me to him.

"You know, I was thinking that our darkest hours aren't our darkest hours—they're our *dawn*," he said, and then he smiled softly when he saw my curious look. "I was sitting here thinking, and I wondered if sometimes those hours are like a light God shines into our hearts, showing us what we are made of . . . what we are made *for*. Think of it," he said. "Jessie, standing by Lillie in spite of her own grief, praying . . . you taking that scripture to them when they needed it the most, even when your heart was so down . . . Jack and Lillie—you all gave your cares to Him, and you *believed*. And look what has come of it, lass . . . look what has come of it." He shook his head in wonder. "'Tis a miracle . . ."

"*My strength is made perfect in weakness . . .*" The words of the scripture Pa had underlined all those years ago whispered to me.

I looked up at the clock we'd hung above the mantle,

saw the time, and turned back to Quinn, feeling love and gratefulness for the gift of such a husband like him that even now is hard to put to words.

"Merry Christmas, Quinn," I said, and those pale blue eyes stared back at me with love and warmth and unshed tears, and I knew he understood.

"Merry Christmas, Callie," he said softly.

I thought I was through writing for the night when Quinn came in and surprised me with a beautiful new headboard for our bed that he had carved special for me; two hearts interlaced with each other so that you can't tell where one ends and the other begins.

"Just like us," he said, smiling softly, and I started crying. It was as if some dam had been broke open by his gift, and I cried about everything. I cried sad for Stem and Jessie, then I cried my relief for little Mercy surviving. Last I cried tears of gratefulness to God for being so faithful even when I had felt almost faithless and for blessing me with a family, with a husband that loved me so . . .

Quinn held me close and kept patting my head, saying, "There, there, lass," and for some odd reason, I suddenly got the picture in my head of him patting Honey's head like that, and I felt myself begin to smile as I looked up at him. A smile that was so long overdue that my face felt almost strange in the pose—but good, too. Quinn seemed to understand.

"I couldn't have asked for a better gift," he said, "than to see you smile like that again."

December 25, 1869 . . .
Christmas Day

And what a joyful day it has been. We had such a good time of it, getting started for town this morning after all the "girls" gathered in our cabin to visit and get things ready while the men set the wagon boxes on the sleds and hitched our teams. Everyone made over Mercy as we worked. She looked perfectly sweet in the little gown Jessie had made for her with its puffed sleeves and fine stitching. Bonny seemed as taken with her as Willa, who couldn't seem to help herself from looking at her again and again. Soon enough, the wagons were filled with straw, hot rocks, and blankets, everyone was bundled up, and off we went through the deep snow. If I wasn't so overjoyed for us all to be together, I might have been scared, for the snow had covered everything so that you couldn't tell where a gully or wash wasn't or the road was. But God smiled on us, and we made it to Audrey in good time.

I admit, I was surprised to see that, in spite of the weather, there was just as great a turnout as there'd been in September—if not more. We filed into Preacher's tent, stomping our feet and grinning at each other like kids. Even Willa seemed pleasantly surprised as she looked around at the crowd clustered around the little wood stove in the middle of the tent. I was amazed that a tent could be filled with such warmth on this icy cold day.

We sang "There Were Shepherds" and "Away in a Manger" then lastly "Silent Night"—which brought the sound of familiar sniffles around the tent.

After the singing, we finally settled down for the

sermon, and I glanced over and smiled, seeing Willa motion to Lillie to ask if she could hold Mercy. Willa kissed Mercy's cheek, so tender, then looked up with a contented smile on her face as Preacher stepped up to the pulpit, and suddenly the smile changed and she looked stunned for some reason.

"I would like to thank everyone for being here today," Preacher began. "It's a hardy bunch that can brave weather such as this, so I hope you'll accept my gift to you this Christmas Day . . . it's the story of a man and a room full of gifts."

There was excited murmurs amongst everyone—especially some of the miners who had been sitting stiff, waiting for the sermon. Children even forgot their squirming and leaned forward in their seats as Preacher began. I felt Willa squirm next to me, but I was already caught up in the picture Preacher had begun to paint of the man who had lived his whole life working and praying but never really living.

He said the man grew old and one day he died, and when he opened his eyes again, he was standing before Jesus. The man was overcome with joy to realize he was in heaven because his life had been so miserable—and he told the Lord as much. Jesus took the man's hand, his smile sad but kind as he led the man into a huge room filled with gifts.

"These were all for you," Jesus said, and the man looked at him, startled. Then he went over to the largest gift, wrapped fine with bows and such, and when he opened it, he saw it was the day of his birth.

The man started tearing into all the boxes then, Preacher told us. He started crying as he saw himself being hugged by a loved one in one of the boxes, heard the laughter of a child in another one. He opened box after box, showing him all the gifts of life—gifts he had never took the time to open . . . never took the time to *see*.

Preacher grew silent for a moment, and I could hear sniffles coming from all over that tent. Then I saw something had caught Preacher's eye, and I saw his eyes widen in surprise, too.

I followed his stare, and I saw Willa suddenly spring up from her seat. She handed Mercy back to Lillie quick, then without a word to any of us, she was out of the tent in a flash. I glanced over at Quinn, who looked as shocked as I felt, then I turned and followed after Willa as fast as I could. I found her just as she was getting ready to step up into her wagon. She must have sensed me, for she looked over her shoulder then. "Please, just go back in, Callie," she said. Seeing her tears, I put my hand on her shoulder softly and asked her what I already knew. Preacher was Willa's long-lost love . . . the man she had waited for to come home from the war.

"All of these years," she said after a while. "Well, *someone* has a sense of humor. Shawn becomes a man of the cloth, and I become the Ringleader of Sin. She laughed then, but there was no humor in her laugh, and I couldn't help thinking it was like watching a delicate piece of crystal fall off a table and you're not sure you can catch it in time before it shatters.

"God's bigger than a bunch of foolish lies," I said. "If it's meant for you and the preacher to be together, there's no one on earth that'll stop it. Least of all you." Willa turned back to me then with a hurt but hopeful look on her face.

"When I saw how that baby was healed I almost believed . . . ," she said softly. Then she frowned. "But if God is real, why doesn't He ever talk to me, Callie? Why didn't He stop me from making such a mess of my life?"

I couldn't help smiling, she sounded so much like me. "We're not puppets, Willa. We have a little thing called choice," I said, then I looked at her close. "Tell me, have you ever really waited—have you tried to listen to see if you'd get an answer?"

"No," she said softly, looking away. "I'm scared." When I asked her what she was scared of, she turned back to me for just a moment.

"Don't you see, Callie?" she said. "If I listen and He doesn't talk—if there really isn't a God—then I really am alone." When she looked at me so sad, it struck me that I was seeing the real Willa Cain for the first time after all the months I had known her . . . a woman who was lonely and so very scared.

"Did it ever occur to you that maybe it was God that brought you here today?" I said. "Wouldn't you like to know if this day is one of your gifts?"

Willa didn't answer me. Instead she climbed onto the seat of her wagon, took up the reins, and hawed her team on down the snowy trail that led out of town . . .

When I turned around, Preacher was standing there, his face grim but determined as he folded his arms across his chest. The rest of the congregation milled behind him, trying to figure out what had caused such a stir, but he didn't seem to notice.

"She should have known better than to run," he said, almost to himself. "I always caught her in the end." He turned and walked back into the tent, the rest of us trailing back in to find our seats again. And as I sat there listening to the deep rise and fall of his voice, as he spoke of what the true gifts were that God had given us, he told us the greatest gift of all was the gift of love. "That was why the Christ Child was born this day," Preacher said, "to give us a chance . . . to give us His love . . ."

Preacher looked down at his Bible then and slowly turned the page. Then he read these words: "And though I have the gift of prophecy, and understand all mysteries, and all knowledge; and though I have all faith, so that I could remove mountains, and have not charity, I am nothing. . . ."

The words made me think of Stem and then of Jessie, how she had kept on loving in spite of her hurt. Then I thought of *all* the people who had loved me—and who I had got to love back—and I thought how poor my life would've been not to have had that love. When I looked at Quinn there was tears in his eyes, and I knew he was thinking the same. I think everyone was feeling that way. There wasn't a dry eye to be found as we all moved slowly out of that tent after the service. There was a difference in the air, too, like everyone had changed somehow in the short space of time. I even overheard Mr. Audrey invite Doc Eddy to their home for Christmas dinner. Mrs. Audrey's smile was wan, but she nodded her agreement just the same.

Pretty soon we had our wagon loaded with Coy and Bonny and her kids, since Willa had already left in the wagon they'd come in. I smiled, seeing the preacher behind us in his own rig with Jessie perched on the seat beside him. As Jack and Lillie took the lead, turning their team down the winding, snow-choked trail that led home,

Quinn and I grinned at each other like kids . . . it *felt* like Christmas. Then I thought of Willa and wished with all my heart she could be with us, too.

It wasn't until we all rumbled into our little valley that I saw my wish had come true. Willa was there, standing by her wagon, shivering, like she had been waiting on us awhile. As I stepped down, I saw her eyes go wide as she spotted Preacher helping Jessie from his buggy. She backed up a little as Preacher headed over to her, but he didn't seem in the least bothered by her reaction.

"I can't think of a better Christmas gift than to be standing here with you, Willa, after all these years," Preacher said, smiling big.

"All these years is right," Willa sniffed. "I guess I should say it's nice to see you're alive, but I'm still trying to figure out how you ended up in the very last place on earth I would imagine *you* to be."

"Don't you see God's hand in this?" he asked, but she refused to look his way.

"No," she said, shaking her head. "I see a poor sense of humor—a bad joke played on the wrong day." Willa paced. "I've decided there are no real happy endings, Shawn Michaels. I've told everyone who would listen that fairy-tale endings were for the weak. Then you show up and try to ruin my speech."

The preacher threw his head back and laughed then. "Same old Willa," he said, then he started to say something else but was overcome with laughter again, and we all found ourselves chuckling, too.

"Go ahead and laugh," Willa said, trying her best not to smile as she looked around at us all. "It was a good speech."

We went inside then to feed our hungry bunch, and after we sang every Christmas song we could remember, we pulled out our surprise for Jessie. She looked up from the stack of goods for quilting, her lips trembling as she thanked each of us. Then it was the children's turn; Patrick gave Jessie a pretty little wooden cross he'd carved for her, and John-Charles gave her a wooden frame with braided horsehair edging for the only picture she had of her and Stem. Sarah and Willie shyly presented her with a little beaded purse. But Rose's gift surprised us all. It was a sampler she'd made for Jessie. "Mrs. Jessie Dawson" was sewn prettily in the middle of a pale piece of linen with a tiny border of flowers and flounces surrounding her name. Hard work for any young girl—but especially for Rose, who avoided sewing like the plague. Amazing what your heart can push you to do.

"I sewed that because you said you never wanted to forget the day you became Mrs. Jessie Dawson," Rose said, a smile hovering on her lips as she waited for Jessie's reaction.

"Why, that's the finest thing I ever seen, sis," Jessie said, smiling past the tears in her eyes. "Thank ye all. Thank ye kindly."

I have a gift to give, too," Preacher announced suddenly. "But it's for Willa." All heads turned to see Willa give a start, looking up from Rose's sampler.

He tried one pocket, and it appeared there was something in it, but he looked like he thought better of pulling it out. Then he went to scrounging in his other pocket, finally coming out with a small square of tissue paper that looked like it had been open and refolded so many times it was near brittle.

He offered the paper to Willa, who looked at it like it might bite her, then he sighed and opened it himself and we saw it was a set of the prettiest hair combs we'd ever seen. They looked to be a green enamel of sorts inlaid with tiny white flowers and vines.

"I meant for you to have these years ago," he said, handing them to her. "For that beautiful raven hair," he added.

Willa touched a hand to her hair, then caught herself. She cleared her throat and looked over at Rose. "Beware of the flatterer," she said. "He feeds you with an empty spoon."

Preacher put his hand to his chest then, as if injured. "Ah, but the thorns which I have reaped are of the tree I planted," he said, smiling.

"He thinks quoting Byron is going to impress me," Willa said to no one in particular, but I saw that her cheeks had turned a pretty pink in spite of her words and a soft smile curved her lips. I looked at Lillie and Jessie, and by their looks, I knew they had seen the same thing.

When I glanced over to Rose, who had been so quiet during this exchange, I saw her lips were pursed and a tiny frown wrinkled her brow as she looked over at Willa, deep in thought, as if the weight of the world were on her mind.

"Miss Willa, why would anyone *feed* you with an empty spoon?" she asked, and we all busted out laughing.

Preacher followed Willa out to her wagon when she abruptly announced it was time for her to go. She had the strangest look on her face, like she was scared to death, but maybe glad, too.

From the window, we watched them talk a bit in the

yard, then we saw her fairly run to her wagon, watched as Preacher stood in the middle of our yard, watching too, until her rig was far out of sight. Then he shook his head and climbed into his buggy, a determined look on his face.

"You know, I was a lot like her when I first met your brother," Lillie said as we turned from the window. "I always told myself if I didn't care, then I wouldn't have to worry about getting hurt again.

"But I cared, no matter how hard I tried. I just had a mask I wore that said I didn't." Lillie shrugged her small shoulders and looked down at Mercy, smiling. "I cared . . . I always cared."

"Well, now we'll just have to say a prayer for that girl, won't we?" Jessie said, looking from Lillie down to Mercy. "Jesus ain't no *suspector* of persons, ye know. A very good friend of mine told me that, and I'm inclined to believe her."

Rose fairly beamed as she looked up into Jessie's smiling face.

"That friend was me, wasn't it, Jessie?"

"It sure was, honey," Jessie said, smiling too, and soon after, we all joined hands to pray.

Are You out there tonight, God? If ever I could imagine You being close enough to look over my shoulder it would be tonight, beneath this huge bowl of cold, clear sky littered with stars . . . Thank You so much for this night, Lord, but if You don't mind my asking one more thing of You, I pray that You help Willa, too. Let what she thinks is her dark hour be her dawn. Let her know You are there, like I do . . . like we all do . . .

Promiseland

Back to work today. I've finally got the cabin back in order and have just finished putting in my last pan of bread. The stack of mending before me is enormous—which is why I chose to take a breath and write—if only for a moment.

No new snowfall, which is good as the cattle were having a hard time of it, figuring out how to dig their noses through the snow to the grass underneath. Rose, our staunch little *horsewoman*, says if it weren't for the cattle watching the horses paw and nose their way to grass, they would have starved "dumb."

Patrick looks like a little bear bundled up as he takes Jasper and Honey out with him to fetch some more wood for me. Jasper and Honey just look none too thrilled about the trip.

Later—Jessie came for dinner this evening. Then, not long after she arrived, Quinn went out for more wood and came back in with Preacher, who said he'd just stopped by for a little visit. A long way through cold and snow for just a little visit, I thought, but I didn't say it. Truth is, we have all taken quite a liking to Preacher. Not just for his preaching, but for the man himself. He has an easy way about him that makes you feel like you've known him forever, so kindhearted and smart, too—not just with books, but life. I could tell Quinn enjoyed his company, too. As I watched them sit and talk in front of the fireplace while Jessie, Rose, and me finished up with the dishes, I couldn't help thinking how they reminded me of two solemn warrior-giants, meeting to talk about the sad ways of humans. I suddenly heard Quinn asking Preacher about his family, and my ears perked up, curious.

"When my family found out I was going west to preach, they thought I'd lost my mind," Preacher said with a wry grin. "My father said, 'You leave, and your money stays.' I told him what I was doing wasn't about money, but he never understood that." Preacher shook his head. "He believed doing anything—or speaking to anyone outside of their 'circle of money'—was going beneath our class."

Quinn looked up from studying his work-worn hands. "Ah," he said. "I imagine your father never played much chess then." Preacher raised a brow, and Quinn grinned. "He would've known, if he had, that the king and the pawn, they go in the same box when the game is over."

Preacher laughed outright then. "I'll have to remember that, McGregor," he said fondly, and Jessie and me smiled at each other. Then there was a knock at the door, and Rose and Patrick ran to open in. *Willa* came in, looking half-froze but pretty in a windblown sort of way. She also looked mortified.

"Well, I didn't know you had company," she said, her eyes sliding Preacher's way, and I saw her put a nervous hand to her hair. "I just thought to come by for a little visit." We all glanced at each other then and grinned.

"I should probably go," she added. "I didn't mean to interrupt anything."

"Well, I do have to be real careful about who I'm seen with," Preacher said with a teasing look, but he stood and offered her his chair.

"You best step lively, then," Willa retorted. "I would

hate to be the cause of your downfall." But she sat down anyway, and as I went to fetch her some coffee, Jessie winked.

"What is it that I hear they call you in town?" he asked.

"Ringleader of Sin," Willa deadpanned, but there was a flicker of hurt in her eyes, too. I knew Preacher saw it, too, for he softened a bit from his teasing her. We all gathered around the fireplace with our chairs and had a good time talking and drinking coffee. But as most good nights do, it came to an end too soon. Rose and Patrick had pleaded for Jessie to be the one to tuck them in, and she went up the ladder behind them with a smile as Preacher and Willa began to bundle up for their trips home. As Quinn and I stood at the door with them I saw Preacher hesitate all of a sudden and turn back to Willa.

"Would tomorrow be too early to call on you?" he asked, and we all turned to see what her answer would be.

Willa looked stunned at first, then some of the wariness eased from her eyes and she laughed. "Are you trying to save me, Shawn Michaels?"

"Maybe," he said smiling—but looking at her thoughtfully, too, before they both headed out the door. "Or maybe God's trying to save us both."

Willa looked back at me for the briefest moment, and a tumble of emotions crossed her face that I had never seen before. "Thank you, Callie," she said, shutting the door behind her.

I told Quinn after they left that I hoped Willa would relent—and soon. That if it was so easy for me to see how much Preacher cared for her, why couldn't she? Quinn just smiled at me, one dark eyebrow raised.

"How soon we forget," he said, and I suddenly felt sheepish, remembering what a time he'd had trying to convince me—and thinking, too, how much I would've lost had I not listened to God instead of myself.

"Maybe God is trying to save us both," Preacher had said.

I pray that You do save them, Lord. I guess I've lived long enough to admit we all need saving from ourselves one time or another in our lives . . .

December 31, 1869 . . .

The eve of our new year . . . Jessie didn't mention that, but I wonder if something in her sensed it was time for a change. If maybe her wanting us to help her pack up some of Stem's things wasn't God's gentle nudge to get her back to the "land of the living," meaning living for *Jessie*—not just us. As Rose and I quickly finished our chores and bundled up to walk the path to Jessie and Stem's place, I couldn't help thinking on that, how Jessie just charged on, helping all of us with no thought to herself. And yet every night she had to trudge back to that cabin and sit alone with her thoughts of what could have been.

Jessie opened the door as quick as I knocked, and it touched my heart to see how eager she was for our company as she ushered us in, taking our coats and herding us over to warm ourselves by the fire. "This place is a sight," she declared, trying to busy herself making coffee as Rose and I glanced around the little cabin that fairly sparkled with neatness. I saw two packing boxes in the corner that looked to be filled with Stem's things, and I wondered what help she was needing when I saw the new quilt that was spread on her bed. It was one of the finest-looking patchwork quilts I've seen. Jessie smiled as Rose and I went over to take a look. Then she joined us, telling us how one day she had been sitting just staring at the quilting frame Stem had made, when she remembered about Lillie's memory quilt.

"I think the Lord brought it to my mind because I was having a hard time thinking of packing his clothes away," Jessie said, smiling. "But that's how He works. I got me a quilt I needed and something of that sweet man's to hold on to when I fall to sleep, too," she added. I saw Rose look up to Jessie then down to the quilt as she bent forward and ran one hand softly over the fabric almost longingly.

Jessie saw the longing, too, for she reached down and took Rose's hand in hers. "I got something for ye, sis," she said, and she led Rose over to the table. Something was hidden there under the tablecloth. Jessie pulled the cloth off, and there sat folded neatly on top of the frame a smaller version of Jessie's own quilt.

"That's yours," Jessie said, and a wide-eyed Rose grabbed up the quilt and hugged it to her chest, the look on her little face so sad and sweet at the same time that it brought tears to my eyes.

"Oh, thank you, Jessie!" Rose said, hugging Jessie's neck while she held tight to the little quilt. "Now we can *both* have something from Stem to hold on to at night."

After we had all dried our eyes, we took to the kitchen and had ourselves some coffee and little sweet cakes Jessie had made. Then Rose shyly asked Jessie if she could look through the boxes of Stem's belongings, and when Jessie said yes, she quickly left us to our talking, quilt clutched tightly in one hand as she sifted through the boxes in the other.

"You didn't have to let her do that, Jessie," I said then, and Jessie sat her cup down and looked at me.

"Why, Callie, it don't hurt me none. Those are just his *things*," she said simply. "Who Stem *was* made up a lot more than them pitiful boxes."

It hit me then, as I glanced back over at those two boxes, maybe that was why they were so meager, that Stem had been so busy in the *doing*, in always helping others, always taking pleasure in *people*, that he'd rarely had need of *things*. I told Jessie I hoped my boxes would be just as small.

"Me, too, honey," Jessie said. "Me too."

Not long after that was when Rose brought us a slip of paper she'd found tucked in one of Stem's old buckskin jackets. She handed the paper to Jessie, and we both watched as Jessie opened it gingerly, squinted her eyes at it, then made as if to tuck it away. I was confused for a moment until it suddenly struck me that maybe she couldn't read.

"It's a mite dark in here," I said so as not to embarrass her. "Maybe we should light that pretty lamp of yours."

"Oh, I'll do it. You hold on to this," she said, fairly shoving the paper into my hand as she pretended to busy herself with the lamp. I opened the paper and glanced at it, then looked up to see Jessie watching me carefully. "Might as well read it," she said, fiddling with her lamp. "Looks like I'll have to add some oil."

"Read it, Mama," Rose said, pleadingly.

I opened the paper gently, then felt a lump come to my

throat as I saw that the date was only two weeks before Stem had died. I touched the indents he'd made with his deliberate, shaky handwriting.

"If yore reading this, then I figger I'm gone. I always did like to have my say, so you might guess I ain't done yet," I read, then I looked up at Rose and Jessie and saw Rose take Jessie's hand, saw a smile tremble on Jessie's lips as she nodded to me. I went on in spite of the lump in my throat. "I ain't no judge, but I figger this can serve as my will. If anyone thinks to dispute it, they kin take it to Quinn McGregor or Jack Wade. They've been like sons to me and know my mind, too. I'm sorry I had to leave you, Jessie, but the one comfort I hav is knowin who I left you *with*. Callie and them have been more family than the folks I was born to. With that sed, I hereby leave all my worldly goods to my wife, Jessie Dawson. They ain't much, but she's loved me better than anyone, and the least I kin do is make sur she's squared away til we see each other agin.

"Lastly, I figger someone had to tell this to Jessie as she can't yet read. I say *yet* not to embarrass her but because I'm countin on her keepin her promise to learn. Not for me, but for herself.

"You never know, Jessie, it might just come in handy one day.

"Love, Stem—or Justice Dawson, for any of them legal types.

"P.S. And tell Rose not to ferget lesson numbr nine hundred."

We all were quiet for a bit—especially Rose, who had walked slowly back over to where the boxes sat. Then, as if a thought suddenly came to her, she came back over to us and took Jessie's hand, asking her if she could be the one to teach her to read.

"Why, that would be right kindly of ye, sis," Jessie said, looking up at me with a distracted kind of smile, and I sensed by the smile that she wanted to be alone in her thoughts for a while. We helped Jessie with the few dishes then began to bundle up again for the walk back home. We hugged each other long and hard. I asked Jessie if she wanted me to take the little letter and read it to the others for her, but she got a funny look on her face and held the paper tight. "If ye don't mind just telling 'em, Callie," she said. "I'd kind of like t' hang on to it for a while." Then she surprised us again by giving Rose one of the boxes of Stem's things.

Rose and I took our leave then, each of us silent in thought as we headed back up the little hill that led to our own cabin. After only a bit, though, I sensed Rose looking up at me as she carried her box along, quilt tucked neatly in at the top, and I smiled down at her.

"So what was lesson nine hundred?" I asked, and Rose cocked her head to one side and smiled up at me with tears in her pale blue eyes.

"When life leaves you bitter, do something to make it better," she recited. "I'm doing it, too," she said proudly. "I'm gonna teach Jessie how to *read*, Mama. I'm *gonna* make it better."

So quiet tonight. Quinn and Patrick were off to bed after the last load of wood. Rose is up in her own bed, "working on something" as I can see the dim light of her lantern still flickering against the cabin walls.

And I write . . . just as I always have, to think, to hope, to remember . . .

January 1, 1870 . . .

Our new year rang in with the sound of an ice storm battering the cabins, bringing us out of our beds and to the windows, where we viewed what looked to be our entire herd standing in the front yard, bawling for help. Quinn and Jack slipped and careened to the barns to gather enough hay to tide them over for a while, then slipped and careened back to the cabins. Quinn is bundling up now for the second round, and I worry about him going out again— he and Jack were very nearly stampeded the *last* time.

Now that the day is nearly done the storm has quit, and Jessie, Lillie, and I have been standing on our porches, calling out to each other from time to time as we are ice-bound. We think the men must have decided to stay in the barn and wait it out until the next round of feeding.

"It seems if it's not people trouble, it's weather trouble. How do ye beat it?" Jessie called out just awhile ago. Lillie held up her hand like an idea had come to her and went back into her cabin. I wonder what she is up to—

Later—Well, now I know what Lillie was up to. We have just come back from our little New Year's celebration down at Jessie's cabin.

It all started when Lillie came back out of her cabin with what looked to be the bottom of one of their packing crates with a rope tied to it. She threw it on the ground, eased herself down to sit on it, reached for the large bundle (Mercy) in John-Charles's arms, and then instructed John-Charles to sit in front of her and hold fast to the rope. Before we could blink, they were headed past our cabin in a flash. "See you at Jessie's, Callie!" she called as I saw a blurred grin go past me and heard John-Charles laughing like I'd never heard him laugh before. Jessie leaned out from her steps, grasping a porch post, and caught them just in time to help stop the contraption.

When pigs fly! I thought at first, then found myself scrounging with Rose and Patrick for one of our packing crates in spite of the thought. Before I knew it, I was sitting down behind Rose and Patrick, wrapping my arms around them tight as we slipped and slid down toward Jessie's cabin on that little scrap of board. I saw Jessie and Lillie standing on the porch, laughing as we headed their way.

Jasper and Honey barked and chased after us, then slid down the hill themselves, legs splayed out like newborn calves. Rose and Patrick whooped for joy, and I felt the laughter begin to bubble up in me, too. Then I heard myself say to Jessie as we came to a stop, "I guess this is how we beat it."

Jessie looked at me, surprised at first, then slapped her leg and laughed. "I guess it is," she said, helping us up and into her warm little cabin.

The men joined us later, and what a good night we all had together . . . and bless Lillie for thinking of such a scheme. Lillie laughed as we bundled up to leave, the men trying their best to scowl over our foolishness, mumbling about us throwing caution to the wind.

"I know Jack thinks I was being reckless," she whispered to us, "but I just wasn't in the mood to give in to another bad day."

We all looked at each other, and it was as if we understood without speaking what Lillie meant by that. I think we all felt we'd had to give in too much already, and as simple as it seemed, our *not* giving in had lifted our spirits, had made us feel like we had a choice again.

"Besides, who is Jack to lecture *us* about being reckless?" I whispered back as I headed out the door with Quinn and the children, and "us girls" couldn't help but chuckle.

The popping, cracking sounds of tree branches breaking and falling to the ground under the weight of the ice and snow echo loudly in the night as I write this. I'd like to imagine it's fireworks that I hear, celebrating our new year . . .

And Lord willing, a new page in our lives.

January 2, 1870 . . .

The Sabbath. The weather has come in almost gentle over the valley today, as if nature is paying its respects to God as well. The sun shines bright, brighter than it has in days, making the Absaroka Mountains look so bold as the sunlight sends slivers of light and warmth across the white blanket of valley.

We have had a good day of prayer and fellowship together, the weather, being as good as it was, seeming to lift our spirits even more.

As Quinn began from the Book of Joshua, I found myself looking out the window as he read, "'So the sun stood still in the midst of heaven, and hasted not to go down about a whole day. And there was no day like that before it or after it, that the LORD hearkened unto the voice of a man: for the LORD fought for Israel.'"

I looked to the sun shining bright over the mountains then turned back to the faces of my family sitting in our cramped little cabin, and I saw that the light of faith had begun to shine bright in their eyes again. And I wondered if it could be possible that God had given us the day as it was to show us His love, to show us He was fighting for us, too.

None of us were exactly "Joshuas," but then, I remember something a very wise little girl reminded us all awhile back.

She said Jesus wasn't a *suspector* of persons . . .

January 3, 1870 . . .

Back to work today. Sunday seems to have not only lifted our spirits, but our energy as well. Quinn is already out and about with Jack, tending to the animals, and I have finished all but my mending for this morning.

Patrick is off to cut wood and check the coop. Rose made a quick job of helping me get the bread kneaded before she was off to help Jessie begin her "learnin' to read."

So much to be done. Ah well, what is it Stem used to say? "*A wishbone ain't no substitute for a backbone.*"

And now I, little journal, must get back to work myself.

Promiseland

January 5, 1870 . . .

Jack and Quinn came in with the news this morning that we lost four head out of the herd. It breaks my heart to hear of any of those poor beasts freezing to death, but the men say it's a very small loss. I'm sure I will get used to being a "cattlewoman," but right now any news of loss is not *small* to me. And yet, there is a new strength in me—in all of us, I think, that keeps us looking past what we see and on to that place where hope for better is . . .

When Quinn came in this afternoon for a quick bite to eat, I noticed he was in one of his talking moods as he mentioned that Rose had told him of the quilt Jessie made, saying he'd never heard of a memory quilt. I told him Lillie's story, then asked if he wanted to see Rose's quilt, and soon we were up and climbing the little ladder to the loft.

We both fell silent as we stared at Rose's bed and discovered what all those nights of her "working on something" were about.

It was the queerest-looking doll I had ever seen: dark burlap face with what looked to be shocks of white horsehair standing out on its head, with a piece of buckskin sewed around its body for a coat. One of its legs was a stick.

"It's Stem," I said, feeling a lump in my throat.

"'Tis enough to spook a man, is what it is," Quinn said, his accent thickening like it always did when he was unsettled. "Looks as if it has the mange . . ."

"It's *Stem*," I said again, and as we looked at the doll we smiled at each other—but neither of us had the heart to laugh. There was something oddly poignant about that odd doll sitting in its place of honor on Jessie's "quilt of memories."

Later—Another snowstorm has blown into the valley tonight, stronger than any we've had so far. Though I hate to admit it, it feels like the storm hasn't just thrown its shadow over the land, but over us as well.

January 6, 1870 . . .

More snow. Worry comes tonight like a hand squeezing our throats, trying to choke our faith . . . our hope. Quinn stood at the window for a long time after dinner, just looking out and not saying a word. He didn't have to. His eyes said enough . . .

He's carving on a piece of wood now, sitting by the fire.

"Mama?" Patrick called from his bed to me this evening as I was writing this. "Yes, Patrick," I said, then there was a brief silence. "That man that was in the fiery furnace with Shadrach, Meshach, and Abednego, that was *Jesus*, wasn't it?"

"Yes," I said and glanced over at Quinn, who had set his carving down and was listening, too.

"Jesus stood in there with them so they wouldn't be scared, didn't He?" This time Patrick didn't wait for my answer, but went on. "Because I know I wouldn't be scared of no fire or *nothing* if Jesus was standing there with me."

"You're right about that, honey," I said, then fell silent for a moment.

I got tears in my eyes, and Quinn did, too, as he looked over at me and whispered, "Out of the mouth of babes, eh, lass?"

All I could do was nod.

How soon we forget to trust, Lord, when some new trouble comes our way . . . And how much more I understand now Your words when You said:

Verily I say unto you,
Whosoever shall not receive the kingdom of God
as a little child shall in no wise enter therein.
—LUKE 18:17

PART THREE

Entering the
Promiseland

Some people were scairt of the gients.
But Joshwa and Kalib wernt.
They knew God was bigger.
So they kept going.

By Rose McGregor
age 9 1/2
Mountana Teritery, 1870

January 7, 1870 . . .

Patrick's sweet words are still ringing in my years, and yet once again we face another trial. I'm almost afraid to write the words, Lord, but You know my heart. I am afraid of what will come of all of this. Of all of us. I'm so weary of trouble, but when I think of quitting it just doesn't seem to be a choice for me anymore. If my steps falter, will You hold my hand and lead me on?

If we weren't living this, if I wasn't seeing it for myself, I would hardly believe another trouble has come to our door so soon.

It all started when Jack and Quinn, seeing a break in the weather, decided to go for supplies this morning and came back with bad news.

It appears that while they were in the mercantile, Jack overheard some part-Indian fellow bragging about being paid to guide a military party against the Blackfeet—declaring to the Audreys that he was going to help see to it that the Blackfeet would be "herded onto a reservation where they belonged."

We all just stood there, looking at Jack, then I glanced over at Lillie, and I never saw her look so scared in all my life. I'd be lying if I said I wasn't scared, too, because I know Jack, and I knew by the way he was avoiding Lillie's eyes that he was going to ride off to warn the Blackfeet before he said it out loud.

"I can't pretend I didn't hear it, Lillie," he said, low, like he was trying to soften the blow of his leaving with his tone. "They're my friends—our boy's *kin*," he added.

"What about us, Jack?" Lillie said, looking down at Mercy sleeping in her arms. "What about *our* family?" She looked up, startled, then, like something had just occurred to her. "You aren't taking John-Charles!" she cried.

We all looked back at Jack again, and he looked down at John-Charles, putting his hand on his son's head. "It might be the only time he'll be able to see them free," he said quietly. Then he asked Quinn if he would help him get the horses ready. Quinn looked over at me with a quick, sorry look then turned to follow Jack out the door.

Just like that, he was going. I knew there was no arguing with him, either. I had seen the look in his eyes before, that kind of faraway look that said he was already gone to the Blackfeet in his mind but was just waiting for his body to catch up.

"Ain't nothin' gonna happen," Jack said, trying to comfort Lillie when he and Quinn came back. "I know where their winter camp is. It'll only be a week, Lillie—two at the most—and then we'll be back home." He hugged her tight to him then, and I saw Lillie relent, and I knew that as mad as she was, it was because she was scared not to let him go.

Jessie and me helped to finish packing the food for him, and the whole time we were wrapping things up, I felt low, like I was helping my brother go to his grave. Jack kissed me on the cheek then grinned at me like he understood. I tried not to cry as I watched him hug Rose and Patrick then Jessie, shaking Quinn's hand before he hugged Lillie to him and kissed Mercy's head. John-Charles waved to everyone like he was going on a picnic, and that made me want to cry even more.

"I thought we had made it, you know?" Lillie said as we

all shivered on the porch together, watching him ride away with John-Charles. "What if he doesn't come back?"

"He'll be back," I said, and as I did, it was like I could hear the sound of my voice mingling with the faraway sound of my mama's. "Our hearts always lead us home."

"Where's home?" Lillie said dully as she turned to me. Her eyes were full of sorrow and doubt, and I saw Jessie reach over and pat her back.

"We're home, honey," Jessie said. "We jes got a little more walkin' to do, is all, to get across that ol' Jordan."

Before they walked off toward their cabins, I heard Lillie ask Jessie if she would mind staying the night with her, and her voice sounded so young and lost it broke my heart to hear it. Jessie, of course, was more than happy to oblige.

I've thought and thought tonight. Thought about all that's happened, about the prayers and the shining moments of seeing answers . . . thought about what Patrick said and Jessie's words, too. I would think after all we've been through, I would've known better than to get so comfortable so soon . . . that I would've remembered that winning a battle doesn't mean you've won the war. And yet I *did* start thinking that way.

All of this talk of our promiseland made me remember what Preacher said about the Israelites and their journey to the Promised Land. Made me remember, too, how downright foolish I thought they were for complaining and getting scared after all God had shown them.

And now, I guess I'm acting no better.

January 8, 1870 . . .

Finished my washing early this morning. I hung everything outside as the sun was shining at first, then by noon a bitter wind began to blow, freezing the clothes, so I brought them back in and have them draped around the fire now.

It is snowing again, and all I can think of is Jack and John-Charles.

Why is it that I can't hear that still, gentle voice that speaks to my heart tonight? I keep paging through my Bible, looking for a scripture to ease my worries . . .

January 10, 1870 . . .

Cold but clear today. Quinn has rode out to Willa's to ask Coy to come help until Jack gets back. Yesterday was the Sabbath, and we spent it reading scriptures and praying. We all are trying our best to keep Lillie's spirits up.

It was so hard—I never have been much of an actress when it comes to hiding my feelings.

I feel so far away from everything, like I'm just going through the motions as my thoughts stray to Jack. My worries. I tried reading scripture again but couldn't seem to find the patience to sit still long enough . . .

I overheard Patrick asking Quinn tonight when John-Charles would be home and heard Quinn telling him soon—that his Uncle Jack knew the calving would be starting shortly and that he hadn't ever left them short-handed yet.

Yet . . .

Jessie and Lillie have been spending a lot of time together, talking, like there's something they share now that they hadn't shared before.

I—no, I won't even think it.

Later—I've just woke up from a dream. I dreamt I was standing alone, surrounded by nothing but blue, when I saw a hand hold something out for me to see. I knew somehow it was Jesus' hand. So I squinted my eyes to try to see what He was holding, and then I realized it was a key of some kind. My only thought was I had to get that key, that it would help me in some way, so I reached forward to take the key, and suddenly Jesus closed His hand over mine, holding it still.

"*I am the key*," He said, and then suddenly I was awake, looking around my room, and now here I sit writing this, Preacher's words coming back to haunt me . . .

"When the trials came, they forgot," he'd said. "They ended up wandering year after year because they forgot God was God."

Thank You for reminding me, Lord. Help me to be strong, to not get so caught up in my worry that I forget You are in charge of all. I pray that You keep Jack and John-Charles in Your loving arms and that You bring them home safely.

January 12, 1870 . . .

Where has the day gone to? I feel like I just opened my eyes, and now it's time to shut them again. I am so tired, but I feel stronger, too, if that makes any sense. I looked in my mirror tonight as I brushed my hair out and was surprised at the woman who stared back at me.

She looked determined, like she could handle just about anything.

January 14, 1870 . . .

From every cut springs new growth, my mama used to say, and though it's the middle of January I feel like we've all been budding in spite of the cold, in spite of our worries for Jack and John-Charles. It's like we've all begun to be of one mind, not just in our work, but most important, in our prayers. Like a row of wheat that springs up out of the ground to reach for the sun at the same exact time . . .

Coy has been helping Quinn quite a bit around the ranch, although he tries to get back to Willa's every chance he can to "help the women." Lillie spends a lot of time between Jessie's and our cabin now, and Mercy gets so much attention Lillie fears she will be "spoiled silly" by the time Jack and John-Charles come home.

Patrick is lost without his cousin. He asks, "When is John-Charles coming back?" so many times that as I write this Rose is telling him to hush. She is taking teaching Jessie to read real serious, her little red head bent down next to Jessie's as they pore over an old reader of hers. "No, Jessie," Rose says, "it sounds like *this*."

Jessie, with her beautiful, old, dark face screwed up in concentration, glances up suddenly, and I see her cock her head to one side as she looks at Rose, sizing her up.

A determined gleam has come to Jessie's eyes, and it's

almost like I can hear her thoughts: *If that little slip of a thing can do it—I can, too.*

And I have no doubt she can.

January 20, 1870 . . .

I was the first to wake this morning and so went to fetch some wood to get breakfast started. I was almost back to the cabin when I had the strong feeling come over me to pray for Jack and his boy. So strong that I took no thought of dropping to my knees in the snow as I bowed my head and prayed.

I'm not sure how long I prayed, but when I opened my eyes I saw Jasper and Honey sitting together right in front of me, just staring. They didn't jump around or try to play as I stood up but followed me quietly back to the house, like they understood.

January 27, 1870 . . .

We have been so hard at work, trying to keep ahead of this bitter weather, that I haven't had a chance to write until now. I have so much to tell you, little journal, and I'm sure you will be as pleased as me to find out it's good news.

Jack and John-Charles have finally come home!

We were laying out some wild hay for the cattle when I saw Quinn kind of cock his head to one side, like he sensed something. Then Coy straightened up and shaded his eyes against the glare of the snow, looking toward the distance. "Rider comin'," was all he said. Then Jessie said excitedly, "It's Jack. I just know it, Callie."

I dropped the hay I had in my hands and pushed my bonnet almost clear off my head so I could see, then I started walking, then running through the snow toward the rider heading into the valley. Even from a distance I could see Jack's wide grin when he spotted me running for him. By the time he trotted up and dismounted to hug me, everyone had surrounded us, laughing and slapping him on the back. John-Charles was so worn out he could just open his eyes a crack to look at Rose and Patrick, then I told my two to run and let Lillie know Jack was home.

We all walked with Jack the rest of the way to his cabin, and as we did, I couldn't help noticing how thin he'd become. But the smile that suddenly appeared on his face when he saw Lillie standing on their front porch with Mercy in her arms was something to behold.

They just stood staring at each other, then Jack turned to lift a sleeping John-Charles from his saddle.

"This the Wade place?" he asked, and I saw Lillie had tears running down her face, but she grinned, too, as she tried to smooth her windblown curls into place quick.

"Sure is," she said as a dimple appeared in her cheek. "You're welcome to come in and try the fare if you like."

"Well now," Jack said. "How do I know it'll be worth the price?"

Lillie shrugged. "You don't. But I guarantee you, it's the only place around that'll give you a square deal," she said, and then they both chuckled like it was an old joke between them.

As I listened to their easy banter, I couldn't help thinking the picture they must have made back in Virginia City: the lady dealer and the gentleman gambler. I told Jessie as much as we stood there, and she nodded.

"I imagine they were a sight," she said as we watched him climb the steps, and he and Lillie shut the door behind them. "Only I never in my life heard tell of a gambler that had tears running down his face like that—unless he lost. And your brother sure don't look like he's lost."

Quinn said tonight I was so pretty in my "happy state" that he would've rode out and carried Jack back on his shoulders if he'd have known the "gude" outcome of it.

"I haven't looked *that* bad, have I?" I asked, and he smiled and wrapped his arms around me.

"It wasn't your looks I was speaking of, lass," he said soft. "'Tis one blessing you Wades have, is that you look good even when things are bad. What I was talking about was your heart, the way your eyes shine your happiness for others. I think I would work double my whole life if I could keep your eyes shining like that."

"You probably will," I said, teasing, and we both laughed. Then we hugged and kissed . . . and well, the rest, little journal, is not for you to know . . .

January 28, 1870 . . .

We have had everyone at our cabin tonight for dinner to celebrate Jack and John-Charles's return. John-Charles seemed so quiet tonight. But it wasn't until our little ones had tuckered themselves out and fell asleep on the floor in front of the fire that we had the chance to hear what had happened on Jack's trip—what happened to John-Charles.

Such a sorrowful, horrible tale . . .

Jack said he and John-Charles had only been with the Indians one night when the military attacked the encampment at daybreak on the *twentieth of January*, the day I'd prayed out in the snow. His voice grew hoarse as he told how the soldiers killed more than 173 Blackfeet, how they captured nearly 140 women and children and led off more than 300 horses. He said the military report was a lie—that they claimed all who were killed were "able-bodied men"—except for fifty or more women and children that were "accidentally killed."

He said, "And I'd like to know how it was 'self-defense' when only one soldier was killed in the battle." Then his face hardened even more, and the muscle in his jaw twitched.

"God forgive me, but I wanted to kill them all for what they did," Jack said then, looking away from us for a moment. "But we were outnumbered and outgunned from the get-go."

Jack said he and John-Charles lay next to Medicine Weasel, John-Charles's grandfather, in the gully to hide. And as they were hiding, he looked down at John-Charles then, expecting him to be hiding his face, but he was looking straight ahead, his eyes growing old as he watched the battle before him. He said when the soldiers had finished and rode away, John-Charles scrambled up the embankment and headed for the village without looking back once. When Jack finally reached the encampment, he said he spotted John-Charles standing in the middle of the smoke and dead bodies littered through camp, just staring. He stared so long and hard Jack said he thought his heart would break for his son.

He looked at all of us, grim, then went on with the

telling of it. Something eerie happened next. He said as he was standing there, he noticed the camp had grown strangely quiet, then out of nowhere a group of horses that had been turned loose came stampeding through the camp. Jack said before he could call out to John-Charles, he was already off and *running* in the midst of the herd. Jack watched him, stunned, unable to reach him, as he ran and ran right along with the wildly pounding horses—and to everyone's amazement after the dust settled, they found him without a single scratch.

Later that night as the elders gathered around the fire, amid the wails of grief and cries for revenge, Jack said the old men kept turning to study John-Charles as he slept peacefully in Jack's lap.

"They told me they had named him Runs-with-Horses and that what he had done was a sign to them," Jack said, "a sign that white men might take their lands—but the white men would never own their hearts."

"Why would they talk like that to *you?*" I said then, and Jack's smile was grim.

"They don't see me as white, Callie," he said, "not after living with them like I did."

But by the troubled look on his face, I knew there was something that had bothered him about it.

Lillie sensed it, too. I saw it in her eyes as she looked over at me, like she had seen, too, that something had been taken from Jack, making him appear suddenly unsure of what might be next.

I saw him watch the fire for a long while, glancing to John-Charles from time to time with such a sad look on his face.

When I finally got the chance to ask him in private what was the matter, he said, "When Raven died, Medicine Weasel told me that no person is ours alone, that they're with us for however long it takes us to learn from them. He told me that's why he wouldn't fight me taking John-Charles away from the tribe. He said there would be things we'd teach each other." Jack ran his hand over his face then, and when he looked at me his eyes were so sad. "But you know what, sis? I think that old man just knew John-Charles would be coming back to him anyway, that maybe all he had to do is wait."

The grief on Jack's face was like he'd already lost John-Charles. As much as I wanted to tell him it surely wasn't that bad, I couldn't.

John-Charles *does* seem changed. I'll never forget the look in his eyes when I hugged him tonight . . . Those green eyes, so much like Jack's, stared back at me with the look of an old man . . . and so distant. Jack and Lillie hadn't missed it, either. I know by the way Jack was so quick to turn and take Mercy from Lillie's arms, like he was already trying to comfort his loss in some way.

Tonight, after everyone had left, I told Quinn it didn't seem fair, after all that Jack had been through, with how hard he'd fought to be a godly man, for this to come to his door now.

"Seems none of us are through battling our giants, yet," Quinn said. "But if any family is up to the fight, I'd say we are." There was a gentling in the lines at his eyes, and he sat down next to me then put his arm around my shoulders, like he always did to comfort me.

Oh Lord, I come to You again and ask that You see us all

through this, that we somehow find Your rest . . . There's so much I hope for my children, for all those I love . . . I guess that's why I understand Jack's worry.

Even as I write this, I wonder if that old Indian was right. Is anyone really ever ours to keep? Even our children? Or are they merely on loan from You, just long enough to see how we'll treat the gift?

May we never lose sight of what a gift each and every one of us is to each other.

January 29, 1870 . . .

Back to work again. Quinn goes to tend the cattle and horses with Jack, Rose milks, and Patrick is off with Jasper and Honey to fetch some more wood. He said to me when he bundled up to go, "Mama, I hope it gets warm soon or we're gonna run out of *trees*."

I can safely say, looking out the window, that I don't think we're in any danger of running out of trees anytime soon.

It is a bright blue day but so cold. White clouds drift around the mountain peeks and seem to hang just above us, almost like you could reach up and touch them . . .

I just spotted John-Charles and Patrick walking toward the woodpile together. They don't appear to be talking much. Patrick has put his arm around John-Charles's shoulder . . . so much like his pa, he seems to sense that sometimes a touch is better than words.

Lillie and me took a trip to Jessie's cabin tonight for a little "mending" party. "Makes a quick work of sewin' when ye have conversation," Jessie said when she'd told us her idea earlier in the day, and we couldn't help but agree. It was a real treat, too, for us to be alone together, to be free to talk and not worry who might hear.

It was no surprise to any of us that as soon as we began to sew, we started talking on all that had happened with Jack and John-Charles.

"Jack's just sick about the whole thing," Lillie said as she jabbed a needle into a pair of worn trousers. "He said he begged Medicine Weasel and some of the others to come with him, but the old man told him he had to see to his people. Now he's just worrying on what it's done to John-Charles to see what he's seen."

"I don't think any of us can imagine what's going on in that little head of his right now," I said as I sewed on one of Rose's dresses.

"You know, I cared for John-Charles that time after his mama was shot . . . when Jack couldn't . . . well, you know. Anyway, sometimes it scared me that he never cried for her. Never cried for nothing, for that matter. He'd just look at me with those eyes of his, like Jack's but different, too . . ." Lillie looked up at me and Jessie then, and I saw the worry in her eyes, and I knew she was wondering what would come of all of it.

"And now I see that look again. Like he knows everything and he hasn't made up his mind whether he likes this world or not."

"Well, honey, I still haven't made up my mind on that, either," Jessie said, looking up from her own sewing, and we all smiled softly at each other. "But one thing I do know for sure is the Lord is faithful, and He's done seen us through so much, He'll see us through this, too."

"If any family is up to the fight, ours is," Quinn had said, and I felt strengthened by the memory of those words. "We just can't give up," I said then. "I remember my mama saying once that life wasn't one long race but a bunch of little ones strung together by time . . . I can't help thinking this is another one we've been given to run."

"Seems like we've been given an awful lot of them races since we've been here, doesn't it?" Lillie said, then she looked between Jessie and me. "Do you ever wonder if God's testing our faith?"

"I've thought on that lately," Jessie said, biting a piece of thread in two. "I don't think He's the one sending the troubles—but I do think He's curious to see what we do with them."

Lillie was quiet for a bit, then I saw her glance away for a moment, a thoughtful look on her face.

"I asked John-Charles to say grace this morning at breakfast, and he said he didn't want to. Said he didn't believe no more. Said he was mad at God. You know what Jack said?" she said softly. "He said, 'You can't be mad at Someone you don't believe in.'"

"What did John-Charles say to that?" Jessie asked, and Lillie smiled a bittersweet kind of smile.

"He said, 'Well, I'm still mad at Him, and you can't change my mind about *that*, Pa!'"

Lillie smiled softly. "All of a sudden I got this real peaceful feeling, and I looked at Jack and said, 'Well, we've been mad before, too, haven't we?' Then he and I bowed our heads and joined hands to pray. You know what? About halfway through Jack saying grace, I felt John-Charles's hand suddenly come to rest on top of ours. All I could think was I had felt just like that before. I mean, how many times have we *all* felt like that, torn between not wanting to believe but knowing deep down He's there, tugging at our angry hearts?"

"Ain't that the truth . . . ," Jessie said. "Ain't that the truth."

I just nodded, and Lillie and Jessie fell silent with me as we went back to sewing. Sometimes the comfort of being with folks that understand the deep-down things in you is enough. Any words after that would've just gotten in the way.

January 30, 1870 . . .

We had a good day, just being together again. Jack read scripture for the Sabbath, ending his reading with a verse he picked from the Song of Solomon: "Many waters cannot quench love, neither can the floods drown it."

I recall it being one of Mama's favorites.

It's funny that it's only now that I'm beginning to understand why she liked it so.

January 31, 1870 . . .

It's been such a mild day for January—which is why we girls took advantage of it—scrubbing our wash *and* our hair, so we could "hang" both out to dry. We had no idea it would cause such a commotion . . .

Lillie and I had been sitting on the porch, letting our hair dry in the sun, when the Indians appeared in our yard out of the blue. We had been talking (I can't even remember what we were saying, now) when I'd happened to turn and saw this old Indian grinning back at me. It struck me odd that his teeth looked so white set in such an old, leathered face. He was dressed in buckskins, wearing what looked to be an ancient pair of cowboy boots on his feet. The young brave standing next to him was a bit stockier, his long hair black instead of silver, but his smile was the same. Next thing we knew, they were stepping up onto our porch, easy as you please.

I'd almost caught my breath when I noticed they weren't really looking at us, but at our *hair*. I saw Lillie put a shaky hand on the arm of her chair as if to rise, but I stopped her. "I'll go get Jack," I said, rising from my own chair. Somewhere around the back of the cabins I could hear the children playing, and I thought to go in the opposite direction. I turned and made like to pass the Indians—and almost succeeded until I felt my hair being grabbed up by strong hands at the nape of my neck. I glanced sideways and saw the older one smiling at me, and I felt the younger one tug on my hair, moving his hands downward, to where my hair fell past the back of my knees. I drew in a deep breath to scream or faint, I'm not sure which one, but then I heard Lillie say, "Why, aren't you—"

Suddenly Jack was there, with Quinn and Coy standing in the yard. I heard Jack say something in a strange language then heard him laugh, and I thought if I wasn't so scared I would have took off after him.

"Callie, that there is Medicine Weasel," Jack said, trying to keep a straight face. I heard the older one say something and then felt the younger brave move his hands off my hair. "One Shot was just measuring your hair," Jack said then. "He ain't ever saw hair so long as yours and Lillie's—but yours is a curiosity. They ain't ever seen red hair."

Jack stepped up on the porch after grasping first Medicine Weasel in a bear hug then the brave called One Shot. Finally he turned and made his introductions. I tried my best to act casual, but the old man stared at me close, then turned and said something to Jack, and they both laughed.

"Medicine Weasel says not to worry, Callie. They don't like to scalp family. It makes for bad feelings."

Well, everyone laughed at that, and I found myself starting to smile too, after I'd gotten over my shock. Pretty soon everyone was filing into our cabin to share some lunch together, and I found myself actually enjoying hearing their laughter as Jack spoke to them then translated for everyone. John-Charles seemed so happy, sitting close to his grandfather's feet as he spoke, but Patrick was almost beside himself with excitement.

"A real live medicine man in our house!" he exclaimed to anyone who would listen, then he turned to his sister. "It's just like in those stories, Rose."

"Oh, Chubs, you're such a *child*," Rose said with all the dignity of a nine-year-old, and we all laughed at that.

We talked and visited all afternoon, Medicine Weasel and One Shot sitting on the floor as they didn't take to chairs for some reason. Then at one point I noticed Medicine Weasel watching us all closely for some time, like he was studying each one of us separately. After a while of that he appeared suddenly satisfied, and I saw him turn and start talking in Blackfoot. I watched Jack's eyes fill up with tears.

"What's he saying?" I asked.

"He says he feels comfortable here," Jack said, listening to the old Indian intently. "He says he thinks we are like the Blackfeet, like him." Jack turned and looked at us then. His smiled was sad. "He says that as he was studying us, he was able to see under our skin and into our spirits, and he saw that our hearts had been broken like his."

The old man looked over at Lillie, who was holding little Mercy in her arms, and he gestured to her. Lillie looked from him to Jack with a little fear in her eyes.

"He's asking to hold her," Jack explained. Then gently he took Mercy from Lillie's arms and placed her into Medicine Weasel's hands. Medicine Weasel looked down at Mercy, and for the second time that day, we saw him smile. He spoke to Jack, and Jack spoke back in the strange tongue, then the old man laughed—a wry kind of laugh.

"He asked her name and what it meant, and when I told him, he said *mercy* is what everyone seeks. He says it's funny he found Mercy in a white man's camp."

Medicine Weasel struggled to his feet and walked slowly over to where Lillie stood. He handed the baby back to her, and when their eyes met, I felt like a kind of peace had settled between them. When he spoke again, it was in English, which startled us all—all but Jack, that is.

"She will give mercy to many," Medicine Weasel said, looking down at the baby and then to John-Charles, who stood close enough to be his shadow. He put his gnarled old hand on top of John-Charles's head with a tenderness that touched my heart. "But she will give the most to her brother."

Our guests have refused the invitation to sleep in the cabins but instead have set to erecting a tepee in the yard—sending the children into whoops of joy.

"Mama, do you think Medicine Weasel would be my grandpa, too?" Rose asked, her face pressed against the window, and it hit me that Rose's curious draw to Medicine Weasel wasn't just because he was an Indian. It was because of losing Stem.

"Me, too," Patrick chimed in, and Rose gave him a look before turning back to me. "Well, Mama?" she said, and I told her I didn't rightly know.

"If you get to, I get to," Patrick said. Rose ignored him until she glanced over and saw the sorrowful look on his little face. I watched her irritation turn to pity, seeing the big bottom lip that stuck out, the pale blue eyes like his pa's, now watery with tears.

"Oh, come on, Chubs, you can sleep with me tonight," she said then, all benevolent. I followed them up the ladder into the loft to tuck them in and watched as Rose set her "doll" off to one side to draw her little memory quilt back and let Patrick in beside her.

Watching Patrick snuggle in with his sister, I thought of how truly blessed we were to have our family together. It made me think, too, of how cruel it was that Medicine Weasel had lost so much of his own family—even his home, by what Jack says. And for no other reason than greed for the land.

After Rose and Patrick finished their prayers, I found myself back downstairs, staring out the window to where Medicine Weasel and One Shot stood with Jack and Quinn, talking. I saw the old Indian glance around to the cabins, then to where some of our cattle were nosing through the snow, and I saw a look come over his face like he was trying to figure something out. His eyes followed the slopes up to the mountains, then back to the valley, and I realized he was wondering why there wasn't room enough for all of us. It was the same kind of look I'd seen on Jessie's face before, like you can't quite understand the cruelty of some people's hearts.

I admit I can't understand it either, and I know God doesn't like it.

What was it Thomas Jefferson said? "Indeed, I tremble for my country when I reflect that God is just."

February 1, 1870 . . .

So bitterly cold today. Rose, Patrick, and John-Charles haven't left the front of the fireplace since they finished their chores this morning. They're playing a game that One Shot taught them, spinning "tops" made of birch wood. Whoever's top, after they smack against each other, can spin the longest, wins.

John-Charles is in the lead, but Rose and Patrick don't seem to mind. I think they're just glad to see him smiling again.

I know I am.

Back to cooking, little journal. We're planning a potluck tonight, and if I don't get to cooking, my *pot* isn't going to be too lucky.

Later—We had such a good time over dinner. Medicine Weasel is about as interesting a person as I have ever met. And, it appears, he was the "talker" of the group tonight.

First thing he shared as he came in was that he didn't "have much respect for cows." He said when they all rode out this morning to check on some of the herd that had drifted toward the slopes, looking for something to eat, he was shocked to see two cows pretty near dead. Just standing there, he said, *starving*.

"Buffalo have better manners than to die like this," he said in English, with a hint of disdain.

"Do Indians believe in God?" Patrick said out of the blue then. Rose tried to nudge him, but I noticed John-Charles looked up at Medicine Weasel, curious to see what he would say.

"Some do," Medicine Weasel replied. He glanced over at Jack and Lillie, then to John-Charles, who was sitting next to him with a considering look on his face.

"Big Plume, a great warrior, told me once how the Lord saved him," he said. Then he smiled, looking over at Jack. "It is a good story."

"We want to hear it, then," Jack said, and everyone agreed.

There was once a young brave, Medicine Weasel told us, who got lost during a raid and ended up alone in the enemy camp. When he realized he was alone, at first he cried, then he remembered about the Lord of the "black robes." As he ran away from the enemy camp, he began to pray. When dawn came he hid in a badger hole until night, then he started running again and praying until morning came, and he hid in the brush, where he fell asleep. As he slept, he dreamed of a handsome white Man who wore a canvas shirt. The Man said to him, "Don't cry, and don't be afraid. You will get home safely." The next morning as he hid and slept, the Man came to him again, this time wearing a blue shirt and saying the same comforting words to him. The third morning, he dreamed of the Man again; this time He wore a red shirt, and He smiled at Big Plume . . .

The fourth time the Man came to him in his dreams was when Big Plume reached the mountains. This time the Man was wearing a skin shirt with holes in it and crosses painted on it. The Man said, "Don't be afraid. I am the Lord, and I am sorry for you. You will get home, and you will live to be an old man."

"As soon as Big Plume made it home, he had a skin shirt made, just like the one he saw in his dream, with holes and red crosses painted on it," Medicine Weasel said. "He wore it in battle and was never injured. When he got too old, he prayed to the Lord and then passed it on to Bear Chief, who also was never injured while wearing it. To this day it is called 'the Lord's shirt.'"

"I sure wish I had that shirt, Grandpa," John-Charles said suddenly, looking up at Medicine Weasel earnestly, and the old man smiled.

"I wish I had that shirt, too," he said with an almost sad note to his voice. Then he looked around the table at all of us. "Big Plume taught me a prayer. Would you like me to say it?"

We all smiled through our tears, nodding as we joined hands around the table, and I saw John-Charles grab first his grandfather's hand, then Lillie's. Medicine Weasel bowed his head and prayed in his humble old voice:

"God Almighty—

"The Blackfeet are all His children.

"He is going to help us on earth;

"If you are good, He will save your soul."

A fine dinner it turned out to be. I think it was the first time in my life I saw someone glad to be wrong. Lillie fairly beamed at Medicine Weasel the rest of the evening, and the poor old fellow, not quite sure why she was doing all that smiling, kept glancing from Jack to One Shot with a puzzled kind of smile, then he'd go back to watching the children spin their tops.

February 3, 1870 . . .

Medicine Weasel still hasn't gotten over my red hair. Tonight after dinner he told Jack he wished for me to give him a lock of it to keep.

I whispered to Jack he could wish all he wanted but he wasn't getting any of my hair, then Jack went and told him and One Shot what I said, and they all had a good laugh about it.

I couldn't help but grin, too, and when my eyes met with Medicine Weasel's, I saw in his look that he was as curious about me as I am about him.

February 7, 1870 . . .

More visitors today. I'm not complaining, though. It's nice to have a break like this to share laughter and food over a warm fire with friends.

Willa, Coy, Bonnie, and the kids were the first to

arrive. Willa stepped down from the wagon, took another look at Medicine Weasel's tepee, and said, "I had a feeling there was something interesting going on."

"Makes ye get up early jes to see what might happen next around here," Jessie laughed, and there was something in her laugh that touched my heart.

I think Jack was worried about an argument breaking out as he's told us the Blackfeet and Crow have always been enemies, but Bonny, Medicine Weasel, and One Shot all got along fine, as if there was a silent understanding between them that they had all lost enough.

Then Preacher arrived, looking surprised but pleased at our crowd as we all once again crowded into our cabin to visit. Medicine Weasel seemed eager for the visit as well, hobbling in behind everyone on his threadbare boots— boots, I'd learned from Jack, that he'd taken in trade all those years ago for nursing Jack back to health.

Rose helped me in the kitchen, and I made tea and some sweet cakes, then put on a pot of beans and had Quinn fetch a chicken for me to bake for later.

When Jack told the story of what happened to the Blackfeet, I saw Willa's face growing suddenly sad, the old doubter in her rearing up again.

"Where is God in that, Shawn?" she asked, glancing over at Medicine Weasel and One Shot, and Preacher shook his head like he'd had the conversation before.

"Those soldiers had a choice," Preacher said. "God gives us that choice—He doesn't want us for puppets, you know."

Willa glanced up with a thoughtful look on her face. "Don't you wish we were—puppets, I mean? Wouldn't it be easier?" she asked, and Preacher looked at her for what seemed a long time.

"No," he said finally. "That would be like forcing someone to do something he doesn't want to do. It wouldn't be real, Willa. You can't force people's will—or their love. It wouldn't be worth much if you did."

We all nodded at the truth of his words—even Willa—and Medicine Weasel, who I know had been listening, chose that moment to turn to Jack and ask him something in Blackfoot.

From the moment Medicine Weasel learned that Preacher was a "holy man," the old Indian had taken a keen interest in what Preacher had to say. So much so that he had chose a spot on the floor close to where Preacher was, for better study of him.

Jack told Preacher then that Medicine Weasel wanted to hear a story from him, and we all smiled. We'd been quick to learn the Blackfeet loved a good story. I remember Jack telling me once that they enjoyed a story better than most anything and would drop whatever they were doing to hear a good tale told. He'd said they figure the work will always be there, but the storyteller might not.

"Why don't you tell us how you got to be a preacher?" Jack asked, and after several of us pleaded, he finally relented.

"Not everyone from the North was good—or the South bad," Preacher started, looking about the faces of our group. His deep voice was both gentle and strong, causing us all to lean in as though we *felt* his words as well as heard them. "Just people caught in a war is all . . .

"I turned bad, though. Seemed the more battles we fought, the more death I saw, the more I drank. I drank and drank, until I wasn't worth much to my men—or to myself.

"One day as I was fixing to start my drinking for the evening, a traveling preacher showed up in our camp. I wasn't too happy about the interruption and decided if I had to be there, I was only going to pretend to listen. Then he starts talking about a war going on . . . a war we couldn't see, a war between God's forces and Satan's. I don't like admitting it now, but I made fun of him. I can't remember what exactly he said to get me to quiet down, but one thing I won't forget is what he told me later as he packed up to leave. He said, 'Son, you got a lot to learn about what's real and what's not. That liquid you pour down your throat isn't real—but God's going to show you what is. He sure is going to show you—and once He does, you aren't ever going to be the same.'"

Preacher was quiet for a bit, then he smiled a wry kind of smile as he glanced over at Willa before going on.

"About a month later, we were in the heat of another battle when I saw one of our boys—his name was Loyal— stand up from behind the barricade. 'Buddy!' he yelled and started running across the field. I saw another soldier then, a Confederate, and his head kind of snapped up, a huge smile broke across his dirty face, and he started running toward us all, yelling, 'Loyal!' over and over. Everything was so confused, with all the smoke and guns going off. One of our men must have thought Buddy was going to kill Loyal . . . he didn't know they were brothers.

"He shot Buddy just as Loyal reached him. But it was

what happened next that I'll never forget as long as I live—none of our men will, if they were ever to admit what they saw. Loyal knelt down, crying, brushing Buddy's hair back from his head, and all of a sudden a stillness came over the whole battlefield. Then all of a sudden, there was these men standing around the two brothers—not soldiers, either, but big men, dressed in simple clothes. And they looked, well, clean—cleaner than anything I've ever seen. One of the big men knelt down next to the brothers, and we saw him take Buddy's hand. Loyal looked right up at the man, tears streaking his face, and said, 'He's going home, ain't he?' The man nodded, and then just like you blinked, they were gone—all but the two brothers—and bullets started flying past us again, smoke pouring across the field like it had never happened . . ."

"What happened to Loyal?" Jack asked, and Preacher smiled a small smile.

"Loyal carried his brother all the way across enemy lines to make sure he would get home for burial, then rejoined our unit that night. Not a scratch on him, either.

"All I could think of that night was that old traveling preacher's words, how God was going to show me what was real. I started thinking if I was going to choose sides, I wanted it to be God's side."

"Angels unaware," Patrick declared, looking up from the circle of children that sat by the fireplace, and we all smiled.

"I believe so, Patrick," Preacher said, nodding, and Patrick beamed at the other children with a satisfied look on his face.

Medicine Weasel sat back, seeming satisfied with the story, too. He turned to Jack and told him in Blackfoot that Preacher's angels made perfect sense to him. Jack told us he'd said if God is our Father, then it was only right that He would send bands of warriors to protect and defend His children.

"It is what any good father would do," Medicine Weasel said finally in English with a shrug of his thin shoulders.

It was then that I turned to see Willa, listening so close she was almost leaning out of her chair. I saw the look on her face, and I could have sworn that it looked like hope. Jessie and Lillie said they saw it, too.

"They say all things work together for good," Jessie said as we stood watching them leave tonight. "But who would have ever thought up a night like this, an old Indian talkin' church as good as Preacher?"

"Well . . . God would!" Lillie said, and we all grinned at each other. Then I said, "Makes you get up early just to see what might happen next around here."

We all laughed. Then Jessie said, "Well, it's truth, ain't it?" then we laughed again, and Jessie shook her head.

"Crazy as loons," she said, shaking her head again, but the way she smiled said she was glad of it.

I'm glad of it, too. I can't help thinking how strange the twists and turns of life's road are, how everything can seem so jumbled and tangled that you're almost sure there's no way to sort it out. Then all of a sudden, a mighty Hand seems to reach down and work those roads smooth so they cross each other at just the right time.

It's funny how the thing Jack and Lillie feared in John-Charles's ties to the Blackfeet is what brought them together closer as a family. I don't think I'll ever forget that old Indian and how he took to Mercy so quick, how with just a few words, he wove a cord that connected them all . . .

and how he spoke of the Lord just when his grandson needed to hear it the most . . .

February 8, 1870 . . .

Quinn and Jack came in this afternoon for a quick cup of coffee and to tell us of our latest loss: One of the cows that had just calved had dropped dead right in front of them. They said that, as fate would have it, another one of the cows had lost a twin the night before, so they had set about the task of trying to get the cow to take to the orphan and nurse it, when they found they had an audience.

Rose and Patrick, they said, soon lost interest and went to feed the horses, but John-Charles stayed on, watching until they were pretty sure the cow was allowing the calf to nurse.

Jack said what unnerved him most was when John-Charles had asked what would happen if the cow decided she only wanted her "real" calf.

"Oh, Jack," Lillie said, looking distressed. "My poor baby has been through so much."

If ever there was any doubt to anyone how much Lillie loved that little boy, it was forever erased by what we saw happen just before dinner as Rose, Patrick, and John-Charles all came tumbling in, their faces red from the cold.

The sudden wary look on John-Charles's face wasn't hard to see as he came skidding to a halt in the front of the room, watching Lillie as she rocked Mercy in her arms.

But Lillie, being Lillie, just looked up from Mercy and smiled at him. "Come on over here, and give your mama a hug," she said softly, and he shook his head, pointing to Mercy.

"Oh, honey," Lillie said. "I have enough room for two."
She shifted Mercy to one side to show him, and after what
seemed an eternity, he finally went to her. "I have room
enough here," Lillie said, pointing to her lap and . . . here,
too." When she pointed to her heart, something in John-
Charles gave, and we watched as he climbed onto her lap
and then leaned his head on her shoulder.

Jack had just carried in a pail of water from the spring for
me. "I don't guess I could love anyone more than I love
Lillie, sis," Jack said, watching the scene, his voice thick
with emotion. I saw him look over at Medicine Weasel, who
was smiling, too, in spite of the tears that stood in his eyes.

Jack crossed the room quickly then, catching Lillie by
surprise as he leaned down and planted a kiss on her lips in
front of us all. I felt like all the stiffness went out of the
room as we chuckled.

Rose said, "Uncle Jack!" turning a shade of pink I never
saw before, but Patrick just smiled.

"Aw, it's okay, Uncle Jack," he said, with a wave of his
hand. "My mama and pa, they do's that all the time."

Everyone had a good laugh at that—except for Rose,
who did her best to look fierce until Jessie put a friendly
arm around her.

"And one day ye'll 'do's' that, too, sis," Jessie chuckled,
and Rose couldn't help but laugh, too.

February 14, 1870 . . .

Patrick's birthday today. It's so hard to imagine my sweet
little fellow being six years old already. I made him his
favorite cake, and Quinn gave him a fine-looking fishing

pole he had made himself. Jessie gave him a little wooden box with a lock on it that had been Stem's, and Jack gave him a little knife that Patrick thought was "first rate."

But Medicine Weasel outdid us all, giving Patrick a beautiful little drum that had bright red fish painted on it and feathers hanging from some of the straps.

No sooner had Patrick started his drumming than Jasper and Honey began to howl woefully to the "music," putting us all in stitches.

John-Charles didn't seem to mind at all as he sat and listened to Lillie, Medicine Weasel, and One Shot talking. But our sweet little Rose was green with envy.

"Can't he see that's hurting their ears," Rose said, a bit grumpily.

Jessie, who knew the green monster when she saw it, went and put her arms once again around Rose's shoulder, and I couldn't help thinking how close the two had become since Rose's decision to teach Jessie to read.

"Now, sis," she said to Rose gently. "Is that any way to carry on? Look at all the good Lord's given ye! Why, ye have a memory quilt *and* a fine doll, and it ain't even yer birthday yet. What's it hurt that yer brother have a little drum to play on?"

I should be used to Rose's moods changing like the wind by now, but she still surprised me—surprised us all—by going over and hugging Patrick.

"I'm sorry, Chubs," she said earnestly, then planted a kiss on his cheek.

Easygoing Patrick just grinned happily. "You were right, Jessie. Now she 'do's' it, too!" he declared, and we all laughed—even Rose.

February 17, 1870 . . .

Another cold day. The men and the boys have been hard at work trying to keep the stock alive, which has left us women to pick up the slack. The need for firewood seems endless, and our "mountain" of larch looks more like a hill now. It's so cold that the firewood sounds as if it's being split when I carry it into the warm cabin. My fingers feel as though they've been split, too, lugging water from the freezing stream, washing clothes that seem to take forever to dry inside the cabin . . . Rose has made me so proud lately, helping with all the chores, then bundling up for the trek down to Jessie's for her lessons. Quinn has decided she needs a "treat" for all of her hard work and is making her a surprise for her birthday this spring that he won't even tell me.

Rose breezed in tonight to tell us that Jessie is coming along "just fine" with her learning. "Jessie does try to get ahead of herself sometimes," she said with a weary sigh as she helped me set the table for dinner. "But I told her patience is a virtue. Isn't that right, Mama?"

I said yes it is—and then pretended to check the biscuits so she couldn't see my grin.

February 18, 1870 . . .

Rose has been coughing up a storm tonight. I've doctored her as best I can, making up a mustard plaster for her chest. Of course, there's no doctor to be had—even if the weather wasn't as bad as it is. It's times like this I feel we are so fragile out here . . .

I think Quinn must have sensed how I was feeling earlier, for he came to me when I was sitting in the rocker, mending and listening for Rose, and he gently took my sewing from me and pulled me to my feet.

"I'm thinking our Rose will be fine, lass," he said softly. "She's made of tough stock, but if it's a doctor you're wishing for, we have one." He took both of my hands in his and smiled. "All we have to do is ask."

We both bowed our heads and prayed, and after we were done, we both looked up at the same time to see Patrick standing at the bottom of the ladder, rubbing his eyes.

"Maybe God will send Rose an *angel unaware* like he did for Mercy and Preacher," he said. He padded across the floor and sat in my lap, looking straight ahead as if he were deep in thought. Then he said, "If God does, Mama, I want to know right away. I don't want to miss it this time."

February 19, 1870 . . .

Our "angel unaware" has turned out to be Medicine Weasel. Not long after Quinn went out to the barn and I had finished up the morning dishes and put another fresh plaster on Rose, I heard a knock at the door and found Jack standing there with Medicine Weasel.

Jack said Medicine Weasel had heard about Rose's cold and offered to doctor her in his tepee. As sick as she was,

Rose hollered a quick, "I want to go, Mama!" from the loft, and soon Jack was carrying her down the ladder for me to bundle her up.

When we turned around, it was as if Medicine Weasel had disappeared. Then I spotted him climbing slowly down the ladder of the loft, holding Rose's "Stem" doll in one of his hands. He looked almost embarrassed to be holding the doll, but I was touched by his thoughtful old heart.

"She'll be in good hands, sis," Jack said, his eyes meeting mine, and I saw the love in them.

"She already is," I told him.

Jessie was beside herself with worry this evening when I told her that Rose had been taken to Medicine Weasel's tepee for doctoring. No matter how much any of us tried to put Jessie's fears at ease, she wasn't having any of it until she saw Rose for herself—which was odd, because Jessie had developed a strange fear of going near the old man's lodge, often walking a wide circle around it most of the time.

"All my fault," Jessie said as we made our way toward Medicine Weasel's tepee. "If that child hadn't come out in the cold every day to help me with my learnin', she wouldn't be so sick."

I tried my best to convince her it wasn't her fault, but it was as if she couldn't listen to me until she saw Rose for herself. Then when we got to the tepee, she told me she'd wait outside, that if Rose could just call out that she was fine, that would suit her.

I entered the tepee and got so caught up with all I saw that I forgot for a moment that Jessie was standing outside in the cold. I was surprised to see there was a settee of sorts propped against one of the hide walls; the dirt floor had been swept neat and had furs and rugs spread across it. I think it was even warmer than our cabins, though the fire in its center was small. I glanced over at Medicine Weasel and One Shot, and they smiled. Then I looked over at Rose, who was snuggled under a thick buffalo robe, her face still looking a bit flushed, but pleased.

I went over and hugged her and asked her how she was feeling, then I told her Jessie was outside, and for her to say something so Jessie could hear her.

"Make sure Jessie doesn't quit her studies, Mama," she said, before breaking down into a fit of coughs, then, louder, "You hear that, Jessie?"

Jessie, who had been standing outside the tepee, wringing her hands in the cold, leaned over and peeked her head just barely through the flap of the door.

"Ye promise to get well, sis," Jessie said, her voice cracking just a bit. "And I'll promise to do them studies. I'll do them *all*, or my name ain't Jessie Dawson."

When I told Quinn tonight what had happened, he just shook his head in wonder.

"I'm thinking she's plucked more than our Jessie's heart-strings," Quinn chuckled. "When I went to check on her this evening, she looked to have about run Medicine Weasel and One Shot ragged with all her questions. The funny thing of it was, they couldn't seem to help themselves, almost like they enjoyed her too much to complain."

We both laughed, then Quinn's eyes turned thoughtful.

"I'm thinking we should be counting our blessing to be in such a caring family," he said softly, and I hugged him then and told him I couldn't agree more.

February 20, 1870 . . .

Sabbath in a tepee . . . who would have ever thought?

February 21, 1870 . . .

Rose is very near well—although I wonder if she will be willing to admit it. When I went to check on her today, she was sitting up with a buffalo robe tucked around her little legs like a tiny queen holding court as Medicine Weasel told a story that sounded to be in part Blackfoot, part English to her, Patrick, and John-Charles.

I had a feeling by the way he waved his hands through the air that he was telling some kind of a war story. "What's that?" I asked, and Rose put her fingers to her lips to shush me. "We're fightin' them dern white-eyes," she said somberly.

Medicine Weasel looked up at me and grinned. I couldn't help grinning, too. "Don't say *dern*, Rose, it isn't nice," I said, and the old Indian gave me a look of something akin to appreciation before he went back to telling the story . . .

February 23, 1870 . . .

Finds Rose home at last. Jessie, bless her heart, seemed happiest of all, spending nearly the whole day up in the little loft talking with Rose. It wasn't until just before she came down to help me get dinner started that I realized how lonely she had been without her little friend, and I felt ashamed that I hadn't seen it sooner.

"I sure did miss our times together, sis," I overheard Jessie say. "I used t' think I liked the quiet, but I don't. Guess having ye with me reminded me of how happy I was when I had my little ones around me."

"Where are they now?" I heard Rose ask.

"Don't rightly know," Jessie said. "But the Lord do, and I reckon I'll jes have to trust Him to watch over 'em."

"I love you, Jessie," Rose said then, and I heard a slight pause. Then, by the sounds, I knew Jessie had leaned over to hug Rose.

"I love you, too, honey," I heard her say, her voice a bit shaky.

It took all I had not to break down crying in front of Jessie as she came down the ladder to help me cook.

Quinn called me outside at sunset to show me something, and I still haven't gotten over the beauty and awe of what we saw.

"I've never seen anything like this," he said as I bundled up and stepped out on our porch next to him then followed his gaze to the sky.

It had been dreary and overcast most of the day, but I noticed a stream of gold light had pressed its way through the clouds forming an upside-down V over one of the mountain peaks, illuminating these tiny ice crystals in the air and making them flash and sparkle with its warmth. Just a breath of a breeze came then, and Quinn said, "Listen." As we did, I could make out a faint tinkling sound, like wind chimes, or the clinking of glass as the ice crystals hit against each other in the breeze.

" 'Tis like the sound of heaven celebrating," Quinn said.

"I wonder what they're celebrating," I said, and Quinn smiled a bit.

"Maybe they're celebrating us, that we've made it this far," he suggested, and I nodded as we both fell silent again to listen.

It was as if in spite of the cold, in spite of the dreary clouds choked with snow that hung above the mountains, God was still showing us He was God. That no matter how dark things could get at times, He would always be there to shine a light through.

February 28, 1870 . . .

Another long day of work, which made our surprise tonight even more special, more worth cherishing forever . . .

I should have known something was up. If Rose's grin was any bigger you wouldn't have seen her face for all the teeth, but I had no idea what was to come until I saw Jessie suddenly stand up after dinner was finished and ask Quinn to see our Bible. She glanced around the table at all of us, and I saw there were tears in her eyes. Then she smiled a big smile at Rose before she opened up the Bible, bent her head, and began to *read*.

" 'In the beginning was the Word, and the Word was

with God and the Word was God.'" She stopped then and closed the book, and only then did she look up at us, great tears of happiness in her eyes.

"Now Jessie Dawson's got the Word, too," she said. "And there ain't no better thing to have, far as I can tell."

PART FOUR

Season of Rest

After God helpd them whip the gients
Joshwa and Kalib wer tired so God
said, "Take A Rest" and they did.

By Rose McGregor
age almost 10
Mountana Teritery, 1870

March 2, 1870 . . .

The promise of spring has tugged us all outside today. The sun is bright, and the snow is melting, pouring off the cabin and barn roofs like little waterfalls, running down the mountainsides and streaming from the branches of the trees like teardrops. It's like the whole valley is weeping—but for grief or joy?

I feel a difference in us with this thaw that's come. Looking to the corrals where the men are working with the horses, I see Quinn take his hat off to wipe his brow, see him glance over to Medicine Weasel and Jack as he tells them something . . . I hear them laugh. One Shot is trotting his horse around the yard, a big smile on his face as he tows a muddy ball of skins behind him with a rope so Rose, Patrick, and John-Charles can try their hands at shooting arrows into a moving target . . . Jessie is sitting next to me here on the porch, rocking Mercy with such a look of love on her sweet old face as Lillie stretches her back and looks to the mountains hooded in blue, smiling . . .

And I, little journal, can't help feeling like we're somehow connected to this land now . . . like our trials have weathered us in the same way winter has weathered the land. And like this land, we are ready for the waters to recede, ready to feel the warm sun shine down upon us again. Ready to feel life again.

If the valley *is* weeping, then it must be for joy . . .

Just found this scripture:

> *In his favour is life: weeping may endure for a night,*
> *but joy cometh in the morning.*
> —Psalm 30:5

It's fitting, I think.

March 3, 1870 . . .

Much excitement with another new calf found in the far meadow today. Patrick and John-Charles came in this afternoon, muddy and grinning, to announce their "find," and I was on the verge of scolding them after an entire morning of cleaning when Patrick said, "And it don't look nothin' like Mercy did when she was born. It's already got hair *and* teeth, too."

I admit I was caught off guard. But there was something so touching in the way the two headed out the door together, talking in earnest over the finer points of being born *with* teeth, that I just didn't have it in my heart to scold them for tracking in mud.

March 4, 1870 . . .

My poetic little "waterfalls" from the other day have turned the valley into a huge bog of mud—mud that's been churned up by our herd of cranky, expectant mothers as we all pitched in to move them in closer this afternoon so as to keep an eye on their calving.

The "ladies" wanted no part of it, of course, and tried every way they could to aggravate our progress, and *I* was trying every way I could to be gentle with them, seeing how poorly they looked after the hard winter.

Though no one spoke it, we were all determined to do anything we could to hang on to what was left of our herd. So the men whistled and hollered, slapping their ropes against their thighs as they herded the contrary cows into the pens. We women helped with the strays and opened and closed the gates as each reluctant mother-to-be was finally cajoled and threatened into entering, and the kids reached through the fence to keep the troughs filled with hay, hoping to soothe the cows' ruffled feelings. Everyone of us was working together as a family, and pretty soon, I felt our spirits rise in spite of the trouble—especially Jack, who watched me with amusement as I tried to shoo one particularly stubborn red heifer away from the thick pool of mire she had just been pulled from. The large brown eyes of hers looking at me so obediently were foolers. No sooner had I got her turned away than she let fly a back leg that would have connected with my head if I hadn't dove out of the way.

Everyone ran to see if I was all right as I landed squarely in a rather large puddle of mud. Once the mud was wiped away and it was determined I would live, Jack teased, "Why, look, I think Callie's met her match—and *she's* got red hair, too!" which caused a hearty round of laughter.

Later—It seems Jack hasn't finished with me, yet. Rose told me in a burst of excitement tonight as she was helping me get dinner ready that "Uncle Jack just named that red cow 'Callie.'" And, she added excitedly, "He said I could name her calf if I wanted and I told him if it was a girl I think 'Tulip' would work. Don't you, Mama?"

"Why not 'Rose'?" I asked dryly, glancing at Quinn, who grinned then pretended to stoke the fire. Rose pursed her lips for a moment in thought.

"Well, I don't want an old cow named after me," Rose

said, sniffing in an almost haughty way. Then, realizing her blunder, she added with a sweet smile, "But *Tulip* is a flower—and that makes it almost like Rose."

I'm thinking that was supposed to make me feel better.

I just woke from a dream of Willa. Oddest dream . . . Willa was running through the mercantile dressed in rags, saying, "I can't find my dress" over and over. Then I saw Preacher, and he was trying to hand her a bolt of white cloth but she wouldn't take it. "It will get dirty if I wear it," Willa said, wringing her hands, and then I woke up.

I wonder what it means. We've been so busy I haven't had a chance to go see her. I pray everything is well with her . . .

March 8, 1870 . . .

The sun just keeps working its wonders on this land, shining over the mountains, tugging leaves from their buds, waking the wildflowers to sing their color through the valley again. Jasper and Honey are so relieved that the snow is gone that they almost look like deer bounding through the valley. Even our cows appear friskier, munching on the new grass for all they're worth—all except for the infamous Callie, who is long overdue and looks so woefully huge she has earned everyone's pity.

Medicine Weasel nearly shocked the life out of me today when I overheard him ask Rose how Callie was doing.

Hard to imagine him being thirty-one already—maybe because I don't want to imagine *me* being twenty-nine. Ah, well, at least we had a good celebration this evening in spite of our "advanced years."

Everyone made a quick work of their chores and gladly gathered at our cabin for the party. With our hens laying again, I was able to make him a sponge cake with icing flavored with just a touch of rose water, and Lillie went all out, making his favorite baked chicken and sweet cornbread. Jessie surprised him with a buckskin shirt of Stem's that she'd worked over to fit him. Quinn gave him a fine box to keep his gun in with a buffalo head carved on the lid that Patrick and John-Charles admired greatly, and Rose proudly presented him with a horsehair whip she'd braided herself.

"But not for Midnight," Rose added. "She's real good at listening now."

Medicine Weasel and One Shot weren't exactly used to the notion of "birthdays" but were eager to celebrate anyway. They gave Jack a saddle made out of buffalo hide that was stuffed with elk hair. It looked odd, but Jack seemed more than pleased to get it.

In spite of all of that, I think it was little Mercy who gave Jack his best gift. We were all laughing and talking when she let out a holler (she's lately discovered she likes the sound of her voice), and Jack went over and picked her up from Lillie, brushing a big but gentle hand over her downy head of curls. She looked up at him with wide eyes and gave him a grin that beat anything I'd seen from a baby that small.

I wish I could describe the delight on Jack's face as he smiled down at her. "Why, bless her little heart, she's smiling at me, Lillie," he said softly, and suddenly we were all crowding around for a look. It was as if Mercy was our living proof, our little bundle of God's grace that would always be there to remind us of that cold winter day a stranger had appeared to show us that we weren't so alone as we thought.

I happened to glance over at Jessie, who was looking down at Mercy with a satisfied look on her face, and I saw Jack suddenly turn toward her, too.

"I sure wish Stem could see her," Jack said gently, and Jessie cocked her head to one side and smiled a kind of half-smile that was full of memories and something I couldn't quite put my finger on.

"Why, I kindly like to imagine he can, Jack," she said softly.

March 22, 1870 . . .

Mild, sunny day today.

Coy showed up at the ranch late this afternoon just as we were finishing up dinner at our outside table. He was grinning before he got off his horse, answering me that Willa was fine and telling us that Preacher would be holding an Easter service in town—but I soon sensed there was more, and Lillie did, too.

"You're looking awful shiny, Coy Harper," she said. "Is there something you have to tell us?"

Coy just laughed and tipped his hat back from his head. "I got some more news," he admitted, then smiled a kind of mischievous smile until Jessie gave him what-for.

"You'd do well to answer 'em quick," Quinn said wryly. "The three of 'em together are a force to be reckoned with." Coy laughed again and then finally announced that he had asked Bonny to marry him—which sent the men into hearty handshakes all around and us girls into several rounds of questions about the wedding plans. So much so I think the poor man's head was swimming with it all by the time he finally took his leave. Jack even said as much, grinning as he stood next to me, watching Coy trot his horse back off toward Willa's again.

"I *am* happy for them," I said then, turning to Jack. "I just hope other folks can be happy for them, too."

Jack nodded and looked at me thoughtfully then, glancing once toward his cabin where Lillie sat on their porch, rocking Mercy and John-Charles side by side, and he smiled softly. "People can get some funny thoughts in their heads sometimes, sis," he said, "about what's right or not. I recall one of the Blackfoot elders pitching a fit when they found out I was marrying Lillie and we'd be the ones to raise John-Charles. He said, 'A fish and a bird can fall in love, but where will they build their nest?'"

Jack's smile was wry. "I knew he was tryin' to say it would never work . . . But it was Medicine Weasel who held up for us. He said there *was* a place for us."

"Where?" I asked, looking up into those green eyes of his and seeing something in them that reminded me of our pa.

Jack smiled then, and he swept his hands through the air, holding them out toward the distance as if he was leading me somewhere special—not with the flashy way of a gambler, but with the way of a man sharing his hard-earned wisdom, the kind of wisdom that comes from someone who has loved, lost, and learned to love again.

"Montana," he said, like he was introducing me to the land for the first time, and we both smiled.

April 7, 1870 . . .

Rose came barreling into the house this evening, tears streaming down her face, hollering that Tulip was going to die if I didn't help. By the time I dried my hands and got out to the yard, I saw that she had rallied the whole family together like a tiny general and set off to lead us to the spot where the newborn calf lay.

When we finally reached the calf, I could see why she was so distraught as the poor thing was too weak to even stand. The strange thing was, the thought of that little calf not making it seemed to grieve us all in a way that I can't quite explain. Before any of us had a chance to say anything, Quinn picked Tulip up and began to carry her to the barn, knowing Callie would follow. The new mother wasn't happy about our carrying off her baby, but as weak as she was she could only trot slowly after Quinn, mooing worriedly for her calf.

First thing we did as soon as we got them into the barn was try to get the calf to nurse, but it was too weak to stand long enough to suck. Jack and Quinn finally held the mama still so I could get some milk from her for the calf, then Jessie made a quick work of fashioning a "teat" like we'd give to a sick baby from a scrap of old cloth, all the while trying to comfort Rose, who was wringing her little hands with worry.

"It's all right, little sis," she said gently, and I was surprised to see Quinn's eyes a mirror image of Rose's worry when I looked up at him.

Once Tulip finally figured out what we were trying to do, she took to the teat quick, bringing whoops of joy from Patrick and John-Charles. We all stood grinning in silence for a while, just watching that little calf perking up with each passing minute, finally standing, then wobbling around on little legs that seemed to point in four directions at once. Even Medicine Weasel managed a smile, pointing to the milk dribbling down her chin, and One Shot laughed.

"She's a sight, ain't she?" Jessie said, stepping back with a relieved smile on her face, and I couldn't help agree.

There is nothing quite like seeing one of God's "newcomers," as Jessie calls them, being given a chance at life . . . and deciding to take it.

April 17, 1870 . . .
Easter Sunday

And a fine Easter it has been. Preacher outdid himself on the service, and giving one of the most beautiful sermons I've ever heard, too. I hope and pray I can remember his words just as he spoke them to us so I can keep them in this journal to read on . . .

We sang "Rock of Ages" and "Amazing Grace," and once we finally got seated, Preacher stepped up to the front. He looked all about the tent, smiling at people, nodding, and as soon as everyone got settled and quiet he began.

"I come from a long line of storytellers, my granddad being the king of the tall tale when we were kids, leaving us laying wide-eyed in our beds at night, dreaming of adventure," Preacher said. "Then there was my Aunt Sadie, who lived such a life in her mind that when she told you of it, you almost doubted the *truth*." Everyone chuckled, and Preacher smiled easily; then his face turned more serious. "There *are* those who use their gift of gab for evil, painting pretty words to hide dark intentions . . . But the best storytellers are those who fire your soul with their words, who leave you with, not just a story to remember, but a different way of looking at *life*—of living life. Jesus was such a man, and it's in His honor that I bring you my story for this Easter Sunday.

"Over the years a lot of folks have asked me the same question: *Why? Why* did He go through with it? *Why* didn't He just call out to God and tell Him to stop all of the madness? After reading the Scriptures more times than I can count, I came to the same answer every time. He did it for love.

"Now remember, this is just a story of sorts. I pray it does justice to His name. So now, I want you to close your eyes, and just imagine . . .

"Imagine Jesus walking up that lonely hill called Calvary . . . . Memories begin to fill Jesus' head as He forces His pain-wracked body on. He stumbles once but rights Himself and continues to walk, remembering. He sees anger, then brokenness and doubt, through the eyes of men desperate for a forgiveness they feared they would never have—the very men who would walk with Him. Then comes the memory of fishing . . . He can hear the slap of a net against the water again, see the childlike amazement on His friend's faces, hear the laughter of a wedding, and remember the loving sister who fell at His feet, weeping pitifully for her brother. So beautiful was the human spirit when it loved . . .

"So many more images come to Him in His memory, and He realizes He has fallen in love with each and every one of them . . . He stumbles again under the heavy burden on His back then feels the grasp of a firm hand and sees His Father's love staring out at Him through the eyes of a man dressed in a soldier's uniform.

"*There are so many who are lost,* He thinks, *so many who need to be found . . . My life for theirs, Father . . .* And with that thought He is given a vision of what would come to pass through the ages. He sees an old man who drinks too much because he's seen too much ugliness in the world. The old man wakes in a snowdrift one night, lying on his back. He begins to cry, calling out for Jesus. A drop of blood falls upon the man, and Jesus sees him being helped up by a scraggly looking boy—a boy who would later give him a Book that would open his eyes to beauty again.

"Jesus takes another step, and as He does, He sees a fallen woman who cries herself to sleep at night when no one else can hear her—but *He* hears—and as she drops to her knees, another drop of blood falls, and suddenly the woman is a laughing mother of four who travels at night to the worst brothels around to tell young girls she understands their life—and she knows Someone who will treat them better—a man called Jesus . . .

"Jesus nods, thinking yes, He understands. Then He lies down willingly as soldiers begin to nail Him to the cross. They begin to hammer, and the pain must be unbearable, but it's as if Jesus is distracted by something. His head is turned, as though He's listening. Somewhere in the distance He can hear the laughter of a child, drowning out the sound of hammering, drowning out the pain, as a lilting little voice sings strong and sweet, echoing throughout the centuries: 'Yes, Jesus loves me . . .'

"As the hours go by, Jesus feels His heart swell with the love that so many would ponder over for years to come. *Why?* they would ask. But, then, they hadn't seen what He had seen. He closes His eyes and with a great sigh, He says the words that would make it happen, the words that would give us a chance to be all God meant for us to be.

"'It is finished.'"

Preacher, who had a distant look on his face as he was telling the story, seemed to come to us then, and he looked around the tent. It was so quiet you could've heard a pin drop.

"But He wasn't *finished* with *us*," Preacher said, his voice thick with emotion, and I saw his eyes travel the crowd, finally coming to rest on Jessie, then all of the rest of our family, and when his eyes caught Willa's, he smiled. "He had only begun to show His love. Peter found that out. I can only imagine how heartbroken he was, sitting in that boat a few days later, tormenting himself over *denying* Jesus. Then he spotted a man standing on the shore. '*It's the Lord!*' he heard John exclaim—and yet he didn't flee. Instead, he plunged into the water and began to swim *toward* Him for all he was worth. Because Peter knew . . .

that no matter how bad he had messed up, he would be forgiven, he would be *loved* . . .

"My prayer for all of you this Easter is that the next time you feeling like running away—you dive into the water instead . . . and that you love each other like Jesus loves us. Love like you've never been hurt before."

Handkerchiefs seemed to suddenly spring up in hands throughout the tent. I heard a lot of sniffing—Willa being one of the snifflers—then I heard someone blow his nose loudly and saw it was the grizzled old southern man that Stem had befriended.

"Ain't never heard the likes," he said to no one in particular. But I'm sure everyone agreed. I glanced up at Preacher, who was walking slowly toward the door of the tent, stopping to shake hands, to pat someone on the back, and I couldn't help thinking, like I always thought when I looked at him, how he didn't quite fit the picture folks had in their minds of a man of the cloth. Willa told me his family had "groomed" him in hopes he'd be a senator or maybe even president one day. Then I remembered the words the old minister had told him, *"God is going to show you what is real, son . . . and once He does, you aren't ever going to be the same . . ."* And I wondered if that man had somehow known what Preacher was meant to be.

Preacher had chosen a beautiful spot for the church's Easter picnic on the outskirts of town, not far from the tent, near a stand of cottonwoods that lined the riverbank. Nearly everyone from the service came, with wagons and buggies spreading out across the hillside as folks started emptying baskets or pails of food and spreading them over sheets and tablecloths spread on the soft spring grass. Like with Preacher's other sermons, kindness seemed to flow out afterward, the haves inviting the have-nots to join in. An odd combination it was to see, but good, too. Preacher stood and called for grace to be said, and it touched my heart, seeing practical strangers join hands to pray.

I know it touched Quinn, too, the way he looked about him as he helped me set the food out on the blanket. It was like Preacher's coming had done more than get us together on the Sabbath. It was knitting us together as a little community, too.

"Fine idea, you had, Preacher," Quinn said after we had all settled our hunger. The Preacher smiled then looked at Willa. "I couldn't have done it without Willa," he said, and she blushed prettily but didn't say a thing—which surprised me.

But it didn't surprise Preacher, for he cleared his throat then. "I told Miss Cain this morning that I had something important I would be telling her today," he said, his smile getting wider. "Which probably explains her pensive silence."

"Oh, for goodness' sakes," Willa said, jumping to her feet as she pretended to dust her skirt off. "You haven't changed a bit—still as ornery as the day is long."

"It's not orneriness—it's spring. And spring is for getting things out in the open, airing them out, so to speak," Preacher said. Patrick and John-Charles, who'd developed a strong liking for Preacher, laughed heartily, like they understood—even though they didn't—and that got everyone else laughing, too.

Preacher stood then, facing Willa, and we all waited with bated breath to see what he was going to do. "As most of you know, I lost most everything I had during the war . . ."

"I have never cared for money; you know that," Willa said suddenly, and he smiled patiently.

"There is one thing I never parted with, though," he went on, looking at all of us then back to Willa. He reached into his pocket and withdrew a handkerchief—a lot like the one he had had at Christmas. Then he silently opened up the handkerchief. We all bent in close to see what he held out, and I felt a lump in my throat as I stared at the single, sparkling diamond that lay in the center of the cloth.

I looked over at Willa, who had been leaning in with the rest of us, and tears were already working their way down her cheeks. She looked up at the preacher and smiled, holding out her hand to turn the little gold ring around on her finger to show the empty setting. She had kept the ring, and he had kept the stone, I thought then. The both of them had never really let go of their love, of their hope that, in spite of miles and hardships, they might be reunited someday.

"You aren't the only one who holds on to things," Willa said thickly, then her breath caught in her throat as we watched Preacher kneel down in front of her.

"I've had to hold these words in me for years, and I'm not holding them in any longer," Preacher said. "Willa Cain, will you marry me?"

I know we were all holding our breaths because as soon as she said yes I heard a huge exhale. Then there was a collective inhale when Preacher asked how long their engagement would be. Willa said, "Long enough," and suddenly that dream I'd had suddenly came to mind for some reason, and I said a quick prayer for them both.

"How long is *that?*" Preacher asked with a tone of frustration we had never heard before, and we all suddenly laughed. Willa did, too.

"Well, not as long as before," she said, grinning, and Preacher couldn't seem to help himself from grinning, too.

When I looked over at Jack, he was grinning as well but seemed to be looking past us all.

"Well, what do you know?" Jack said as he rocked Mercy in his arms. "Here comes ol' Mother Long herself."

Lillie whispered, "Shame on you," as we turned to see Mrs. Audrey and her brood coming toward us. "I wonder if I should do my wolf howl," Jack added under his breath, grinning. Quinn, Jessie, and I were quick to look away so as not to laugh. Anyone who's been around Jack long enough knows he has that affect on you.

Preacher looked curious enough to ask, but then Mrs. Audrey, Mrs. Pumphrey, and Mrs. Spence were nearing, looking like they had a specific purpose in mind. All but Mr. Audrey. He just looked uncomfortable, like he wasn't sure what was going to happen.

Mrs. Audrey nodded to us all briefly before turning to Preacher. "Quite a little group you have here, Preacher," she said, and he just smiled.

"So, you've already met my friends then?" Preacher said evenly, and there was such a genuine kindness to his words that Mrs. Audrey's face suddenly got a bit contrite, like she was trying to figure which way to lean. Mrs. Pumphrey nudged her, but Mrs. Audrey was looking to where Coy and Bonny sat, watching the children play near the banks of the river.

"Why, isn't that Mr. Carey's sq—," she started, but then Mr. Audrey nudged her, too, and she said, "For goodness' sakes, Percy!"

Then Mrs. Pumphrey cleared her throat. "What Leah is trying to say, Preacher, is your preaching has done us all some good—enough that we know it's high time we started acting better toward our *neighbors* and all . . ."

Suddenly Mrs. Pumphrey seemed to lose steam—not to mention words.

"'Do unto others as you would have them do unto you' is what we should've been practicing all along," Mrs. Spence said, as clear as a bell, shocking us all. "I just hope it ain't too late."

"Hear, hear," Mr. Audrey said then—another shock. He glanced toward his wife and the rest of the group then back to Preacher, squaring his small shoulders a bit as he said a quick "Have a good day, now," even smiling at the rest of us before he turned away to follow the rest of them as they quickly made their way back to where their wagon was waiting.

"Why, Preacher," Jessie said, breaking the silence, "I think the Lord's showing ye that all yer hard work is startin' to pay off."

Preacher looked dazed for a moment, then grateful, and then a soft smile formed on his handsome face. He glanced over at Willa.

"In more ways than one," he said.

As I read over what I just wrote, I can't help thinking that it hasn't been just Preacher's words but his ways that has touched us all. Seeing how kindly he treated Mrs. Audrey and her group in spite of their troublesome behavior didn't just touch my heart. It also taught me something, too, made me want to be more like Preacher, too.

I told Quinn tonight that it just goes to show that sometimes we *are* the only Bible some folks will ever have a chance to read. He smiled softly.

"And what a tragedy our lives are," he said, "if we never allow them to do so, lass."

May 2, 1870 . . .

It has been raining nearly all day. But the thick, gray storm clouds hanging over the mountain peaks haven't dampened our spirits at all. As a matter of fact, I've wondered often today if us girls aren't as excited as the bride- and groom-to-be with all the fun we've had, decorating for the wedding tomorrow.

We've swept and cleaned the barn out as best as we could and made an archway with greenery in the center above the door for the bride and groom to walk under. Then we had the men set up some makeshift tables and spread fine-looking linen cloths over them for the food. Rose, thankfully, gathered as many bunches of wildflowers as she could find this morning before the rain, and we've placed them all around the inside of the barn in little cups and tins of water, and it's looking almost pretty in a quaint kind of way.

Mr. Audrey came out to deliver the rest of the supplies Quinn and Jack had ordered, and in wanting to practice brotherly love, we decided Coy and Bonny would want us to invite the Audreys to the wedding (which seemed to please Mr. Audrey a lot). We told them to bring Mrs. Pumphrey and Mrs. Spence, too.

And now, little journal, I am off to do some cooking.

I pray as I put the finish to this page that Coy and Bonny will be as blessed as Quinn and I in their new life together and that the Lord leads them always.

Because I can't imagine anything better than that.

May 5, 1870 . . .

What a beautiful wedding day for Coy and Bonny—and not just in weather but in spirit also. As I watched the two of them standing before Preacher today, Bonny looking so pretty in her beautiful antelope-skin dress and the little sprays of flowers Willa had tucked into her hair, and Coy, so handsome and strong, his dark face beaming love, I couldn't help being awed by the beauty of the moment. There is something poetic, almost like hearing a sweet song for the first time, seeing how God is able to put souls together that link so perfectly.

Coy and Bonny, two people so different yet so alike, both so alone in the world . . . so willing to take a chance at love.

We were all beaming happiness for them as Preacher read from Scripture about love. The Audreys, Mrs. Pumphrey, and Mrs. Spence were almost decent, and Mrs. Pumphrey even got a little teary-eyed when Bonny shyly said, "I do."

About the only time I felt sad was when the old-timer Willa knew struck up his fiddle-playing for a dance. I felt a sharp, bittersweet pain go through me then, remembering Stem playing his fiddle the very first time Quinn and I danced together. He'd taken the fiddle from some young fellow trying to scratch out a tune saying, *"Give me that fiddle, son! Yer playing them strings like they's still in the cat!"* How we'd all laughed, then smiled with joy, as he played a tune slow and sweet.

Memories of Stem seemed to be with everyone as I looked around our barn.

I saw Coy and his new bride look at each other when the music started. Coy bent over and whispered something in Bonny's ear, and I saw her nod and smile. Then Coy turned and walked slowly over to the corner where Jessie sat, her eyes closed with a kind of sad smile on her face.

I saw Coy reach down and gently take Jessie's hand, and she opened her eyes in surprise then smiled as he drew her up and into his bearlike arms. They turned round and round across the swept dirt dance floor, and I felt tears come to my eyes as I watched Coy press his hand gently against Jessie's back and saw how Jessie closed her eyes with such a sweet smile of pleasure and gratefulness for that touch—the kind of human touch we were all meant to give, I think. And it hit me with the memory of what Lillie had said all those months back about how frail we really are. But I remembered, too, what the Good Book says about love never failing . . .

And it didn't—didn't fail us once as we laughed and celebrated long into the evening, twirling round and round that dusty dirt floor of the barn as the sun set in golden glory behind the mountains in the distance.

Quinn was stoking a small fire in the fireplace as I was writing this, and when I looked up at him, his face was so deep in thought that I asked him what was the matter.

"If you could turn back the page, lass, would you do it the same?" he asked then, his pale blue eyes searching my face. "Would you marry me again?"

"No," I said abruptly, then grinned as Quinn's head snapped around to look at me, and I laughed. "I would've married you sooner," I added. "After all, I know how it all turns out now."

Quinn grinned. "And you wonder where Rose gets her ways," he said, chuckling as he leaned down and kissed the tip of my nose. Then he whispered in my ear, "But you can't know how it *all* turns out—we've only just begun."

May 6, 1870

My sweet Rose's birthday today . . . If ever there was a girl who's loved, it's our Rose. Seems all of Montana Territory showed up just to let her know that, too.

Once the table was set, we all joined hands and sang, and somewhere in our song, Quinn's eyes met mine, and the love and pride in them for our daughter made me remember what he'd said the night before about not knowing how it'd all turn out. It hit me then that the knowing of it didn't matter so much anymore—that being together, being loved, was all that really mattered.

Rose beamed bigger than I'd ever seen, hanging onto

the little journal I gave her in one hand as she opened the rest of her gifts.

But it was her Pa's gift that made her cry.

She had just finished opening the last of the gifts when Quinn stood and smiled softly at her, then he went out the door without another word. We all knew something was about to happen, so we crowded out onto the porch to watch. Soon we saw Quinn leading Midnight from the barn, smiling softly as he neared Rose, who was waiting patiently on the bottom step of the porch.

"Fair Rose," he said, his voice thick with emotion. "T'day Midnight is officially yours—and the saddle too, lass. But not so you can ride away from us—so you will always have a way to get home."

We all watched with tears in our eyes as Rose looked first at Midnight with such love and then to the saddle that Quinn had spent so many hours hand-tooling himself. Then, much to our surprise, Rose walked right past her gift and over to Quinn. She grabbed his hands, rubbing her small fingers over the cracks and calluses, over the new scratches that lined his work-worn palms.

"I love you so much, Pa," she said, tears streaming down her small face, and I saw everyone glancing at each other in surprise at Rose's reaction.

I wasn't surprised, though. Because I knew as much as my daughter loved that horse and the new saddle, she loved her pa more.

May 8, 1870 . . .

I have been thinking all day on this. Through cleaning and cooking, lugging water from the stream, those words of Preacher's has come to me over and over about us loving like we've never been hurt before. I thought of how hurt I was when Pa and our sister Rose died and how I almost didn't marry Quinn because of the hurt. Then I thought of Jack and Lillie, of Bonny, then Willa, wanting so bad to believe but struggling against her fear, and of Jessie pressing on in spite of it . . .

And I couldn't help but wonder if all we have been through was part of finding our promiseland—and I don't mean a place, but our promiseland *inside* of ourselves.

If maybe once we learn to love like the Lord loves us, like we've never been hurt before, then that's when we find our home . . . our promiseland . . .

May 9, 1870 . . .

Another warm day, which found me making several trips to the stream, the last of which was when I found John-Charles there. He was standing near the banks as he stared off to the distance, and though I knew he sensed me, he didn't turn around right off. When I followed his gaze, I understood why. The wild horses had returned, spread out across the meadow in a breathtaking blanket of color as they tossed their heads and whinnied from the opposite side of the stream.

"They're so beautiful," I said, almost to myself, and I saw John-Charles turn to look at me then.

"Yeah," he said, then looked at me close, like he was wondering if he could trust me with something.

"They let me pet 'em," he said finally. Then I saw him glance over his shoulder quick. "I don't tell Pa, though. He'd want to catch 'em." His eyes grew thoughtful as he looked back out toward the herd, and something about the way he looked made me think of Jack when he was young. "They were here first. They should be free."

For some reason I sensed he wasn't just talking of the horses—but of his mama's people . . . of his grandfather who would soon be leaving for the reservation to search for whatever family they might have left.

"They *should* be free," I said, and he smiled at me almost like he was seeing me for the first time.

Before we could talk anymore, Patrick showed up with their fishing poles, and John-Charles was waving good-bye to me as he ran to catch up with his cousin, a little boy again, looking forward to a day of fishing.

I stayed out there for a while after they tromped off down the stream to their "secret" fishing hole, drinking in the beauty of the land and of the wild horses that were as much a part of the land as the mountains that stood dark against the brilliant blue sky.

I know the horses sensed me, but for some reason this time they didn't run off right away but lingered. I saw the leader of the herd toss his head then, and for a moment, I almost imagined he looked right at me before he whinnied and the rest of the herd turned to follow him as he began to slowly trot away. I watched them until they were far out of sight, and for the first time since we came to this land, to Montana, I felt I had been accepted in a way.

Felt maybe I was no longer a trespasser . . .

Blessed be the LORD, that hath given rest unto his people Israel, according to all that he promised: there hath not failed

Promiseland

one word of all his good promise, which he promised by the hand of Moses his servant.

— 1 KINGS 8:56

May 11, 1870...

I found Jessie in her garden this morning—or, I should say, I heard her first, for her deep voice carried across the valley as I was walking back from the henhouse with my apron full of eggs, and I stopped for a moment to listen to her sing. I'd never heard the song before, but it was beautiful, full of hope as she sang about loved ones waiting for us on the other side of the river... Though I couldn't help smiling to myself when I finally spotted her, hunched over, her skirts swaying sideways as she sang and tilled the ground.

Jessie looked up then and smiled good-naturedly. "I'm sure I'm a sight," she said, pushing back her bonnet. Then she stretched her back and looked out over the land, her eyes turning thoughtful.

She said, "Remember when I told ye I like to stay outside because I felt closer to Stem somehow? Well, all these months I never felt him once, no matter how long I'd stand outside." Jessie shook her head. "This morning I woke up, and I decided I was gonna come tend this here garden for *me*. No more looking or waiting, I said. I come for me, just to feel my hands in the dirt, feel the sun."

Jessie looked over at me with a shy kind of smile. "I was hunkered down over these here rows, Callie, and I know it sounds crazy but I could've sworn I heard Stem. He say, "Bout time, old woman. Ye ain't been waitin' on the Lord? Well, He's been waitin' on *you*.'" She cocked her head sideways. "Now, what do ye think that means, Callie?"

"I don't know," I said slowly, then I found myself grinning. "But it might be fun to find out, don't you think?"

Jessie chuckled. "You are something else." She gazed up at the sky for a long moment, then she reached over and pointed to a new sprout of what looked to be tomatoes. "Wasn't no more than a tiny green spot over a week ago," she said. "Sure is somethin' to watch things grow, ain't it?"

I found myself crouching down in the dirt to have a look and felt the same awe I'd always felt seeing that first tiny shoot of a plant begin its life. "It has always amazed me, seeing something grow so big from such a little seed planted in the dirt," I said then, and Jessie cocked her head to one side again and looked at me like some thought had just occurred to her.

"Kindly like a tiny miracle, ain't it?" she said.

She smiled at me then, a warm comforting smile that seemed a mile wide, and I smiled, too, thinking her smile, to me, felt just like summer.

We had a fine string of trout that we pan-fried for supper tonight, and Patrick, so deliriously happy to have been the one who caught them, is already after Quinn to take him fishing again in the morning.

"We'll go if we get up early enough in the morning, lad, so to finish our chores," Quinn said, smiling. "'Tis the early bird that gets the worm, you know."

"Oh, I know, Pa," Patrick said with a grin. "I saved them in here so that bird *wouldn't* get them."

He dug into the pocket of his trouser and produced a handful of some very wilted-looking worms for us to see. Rose tried to poke fun, but he was having none of it, turning his back to her as he looked up at Quinn so seriously.

"They'll do, right Pa?" he asked, and Quinn bent down, pretending to inspect them in earnest, and I was struck as I watched the two of them with their dark heads bent together, how much alike they really were.

"They'll do," Quinn announced finally, and when he looked up at me, his pale blue eyes were filled with a little laughter—and a whole lot of love.

May 12, 1870 . . .

Mr. Audrey paid us a visit today. But what surprised us even more than his visit was the letter he had carried all the way out to the ranch for *Jessie*. It appears our Stem, or "Justice Dawson," had spent a great deal of money, placing ads in newspapers all over the country, telling of Jessie's search for her family. And there's no doubt in any of our minds that it was God who made sure her family found them.

"He's never early, never late . . . but always on time," Jessie said as she looked up at me after reading through the letter from her eldest daughter for a second time. "Canada— can ye imagine that? The good Lord knew, He *knew*, I was to read this here letter myself, Callie." Jessie began to cry then, and I did, too, tears running down both of our cheeks as we stood together on the front porch of her cabin.

"He put Stem after me to learn to read . . . then had our little sis help me finish with it. I never could figure out why it was so important for an old woman like me to learn readin' . . . But now I know. Yes, Lord, I surely know . . ."

Jessie pressed the letter to her heart gently, her large brown eyes filling with tears once more as she looked toward the distance where the little grave sat beneath two towering willows. "Oh, Stem. Oh, my sweet man," she said, smiling and crying at the same time, and I was struck how I had never seen such a beautiful face in my life.

None of us could think of anything else but Jessie's letter tonight, as excited as we all are for her.

Jack said, "What are the odds?" as he shook his head in wonder for what seemed the twentieth time, and Lillie looked up from rocking Mercy with a smile.

"Jack," she said. "You and I, of all people, could testify to just how much God likes to show folks He tends to favor those with bad odds—kind of leaves them no doubt of Who's really in charge."

May 13, 1870 . . .

It's been decided that Quinn and I will be the ones to take Jessie to Helena. Her daughter's letter says they all plan to arrive on the twentieth, so that gives us a week to get there, and I have never seen a more excited person in my life.

Jessie has come up to the cabin at least four times already as I was packing to ask me if I thought "this dress" or "this bonnet" would look better for meeting them at the train.

Rose and Patrick aren't too happy at being left behind. They have joined forces, sitting side by side to grace Quinn and me with their injured looks.

Promiseland

May 14, 1870 ...

We are off! May God grant us a safe journey.

May 19, 1870 ...

We've only just made it into Helena, and it's the first time
I've had a chance to sit and write. This city is such a surprise after living out in the valley so long. There are people
everywhere, wagons and buggies on a constant move up
and down the streets as I gaze out this window of the hotel
we're staying at—so many storehouses and cabins, saloons
and gambling dens, the sounds of saws and hammers
working at even this late hour. The odd thing is, I'd
thought I would enjoy seeing so many people again, but I
find myself missing home instead, missing the valley and
watching the sun set behind the mountains . . . missing
our little ones.

I guess that's why the sight of Jessie rocking in that
rocker on the front porch of this hotel seems so touching.
When Quinn came back from checking on some buyers
for our cattle, we joined Jessie on the porch, and I soon
saw a smile come to Quinn's face as he watched her
rocking back and forth for all she was worth.

"I'm thinking if that rocker had wheels, Jessie," he
teased, "you'd already be back to the valley by now."

Jessie grinned big, but there was a determined look on
her face, too—the look of a mother who would die before
she lost her children another time.

"No sir, I won't be leavin' jes yet," she said after a while.
"Not without my babies, I won't."

May 20, 1870 . . .

We took Jessie to the train station in Helena today, and I think I was as nervous as Jessie as she stood as still as a statue, watching for that train to pull in. Just as the train neared us, a heavy rain began to fall, pouring from the sky, but Jessie stood her ground—and so did I.

Through the sheet of rain I watched the train come to a halt and saw the conductor open the door. That's when I spotted a young woman of about my age as she fairly burst through that door and down the steps with what looked like the rest of her family pouring forth after her. I heard Jessie cry out the woman's name then, like it was the only name on earth, and I started crying when I heard that young woman yell, "Mama! Oh, my mama!"

They ran to each other, hugging and crying, and as the rest of Jessie's long-lost family surrounded her, those words that the stranger had spoke to Jessie all those months ago came to me like a whisper: *"Blessed are they that mourn, for they shall be comforted . . ."*

They all hugged each other tight, swaying together as the rain poured down around them so hard that they slipped and fell in the mud. But they only laughed harder, not caring about the rain or the mud.

I didn't care, either. Because I knew God *had* heard Jessie's prayers all along. Heard all our prayers, really. And somewhere up there, I just knew there was a certain angel looking on as an old man dressed in buckskins stood with a smile on his face a mile wide, holding his hand out to Jesus . . . And Jesus taking that hand, saying with a chuckle,

"Well done, thou good and faithful servant."

May 28, 1870 . . .

It feels so good to be back home I don't think I ever want to leave again. What surprises me more is that I think our children have decided they don't, either . . .

Earlier, as I was hanging some of the wash out to dry, I spotted Rose, Patrick, and John-Charles all tromping up the hill behind the cabins, Jasper and Honey trotting close behind. And as I heard their voices carrying in the clear air, I stopped what I was doing to watch them. There was something about the way they walked together . . . I don't know . . . like they weren't new to the land anymore, but born to it, and I couldn't help thinking it was as if their roots had been sown deep—not by time, but by the struggles they had endured alongside the rest of us . . .

"Jessie says living out here will give us gumption," Rose was saying as she spread a blanket down for them to lie on at the top of the hill. I saw Patrick hesitate then, looking around the grass. Rose looked, too. "What are you doing?" she said, and he looked up at her.

"I already had gumption once," he said. "And it made my legs itch. I don't want it again if I can help it." John-Charles started looking around warily then, and Rose laughed.

"You sillies," she said. "Gumption means you stick to something even if it gets hard."

John-Charles nodded thoughtfully, and Patrick said, "Like Jessie learnin' to read?" I heard Rose tell him yes as they all three plopped down on the blanket, Rose in the middle, as the talk soon turned to the business of making out shapes from the clouds.

"That one there looks like a buffalo's head," Rose said, starting the game, "and over there is a man's face. He looks just like he's smiling."

Jasper barked then, and Patrick said, "Look, Jasper sees a squirrel."

"Well, that one looks like a cow chip," John-Charles teased, and both boys laughed boisterously. Rose laughed, too, then she sighed.

"I wonder what I'll be when I grow up," she said out of the blue as she peered up at the sky.

"I just want to be here," John-Charles said, then Rose sat up and looked at him, and Patrick did, too.

"You can't be a *place*," she said indignantly, but John-Charles made like to wave her off.

"I can be anything I want to," he said, reminding me so much of Jack as he plucked a blade of grass then and put it in his mouth.

"I want to be *here*," he said again, "with the mountains and the horses. I don't think I ever want to leave."

"Me, either," Patrick said with a surge of conviction, lying back down. Rose followed, looking up at the sky again.

"I don't want to leave either," she said softly. "I want to be here 'til I die, then I want to be buried next to Stem. On his left side, though—Jessie says she gets the right side 'cause of holy matrimony."

They went on talking like that for a goodly while, and as I went back to hanging out clothes, I felt tears spring to my eyes, realizing that somehow along the way, our three little ones had formed a bond among themselves that was more than just blood.

When the men trailed in this evening, I heard the same sound in their voices, too, heard it in Jessie's low, sweet voice as she proudly read Scripture this evening, looking up from time to time to her children and grandbabies. I saw it in Lillie's peaceful eyes as she handed Mercy to me to hold. I saw it in Medicine Weasel's smile as he hugged John-Charles to him and patted him on the head with a gnarled old hand.

Quinn looked at me and smiled then with such a love, and I felt it roll over my heart like a warm balm. And suddenly I heard something whisper deep within me, telling me that balm was God, spreading His love over us just like the sun had soothed the winter-weary land, knitting us into the family we were always meant to be.

June 1, 1870 . . .

My last page, little journal . . . soon I will be opening the new one Quinn has brought home from the mercantile. Funny, but I feel almost like I'm leaving an old friend behind as I take a last look at these pages that have kept my thoughts such company over these past months. So *much* has happened . . . and yet I look forward to what's to come.

I feel a quietness in us all now, like we've all, in our own way, begun to make our peace with God, begun to trust Him with not just a bit of our lives but with *all* of our lives . . .

Christians, having to make peace with God? I can hear some say, but then I don't imagine they're being truthful in their hearts if they ask such a thing. If they were, they'd know it's just part of the journey. They'd know what it takes to learn going through the worst of times can make you a better person for it, can make you see things you would've never seen in the good times. They'd know that making peace doesn't mean forgetting . . .

I don't think He *wants* us to forget. For if we forget the storm, how can we relish the calm that comes after?

Of course, I'm not so foolish as to think this is the end, either—but I do think it's a new page of our lives.

There is still so much more work to be done . . . but I refuse to complain. We're a *family* now, a real family that has its ups and downs but that also has its times of joy, too, and I can't think of a finer gift from God than that.

I don't think I'll ever forget the look of sheer happiness on Jessie's face tonight at dinner, surrounded by her daughter and two sons and their families . . . of Coy and Bonny holding hands as they walked down by the stream together . . . or of Willa and Preacher catching each other's eyes just before Preacher bowed his head and said grace over our dinner.

And what a spread it was! Jack couldn't help himself from teasing Jessie, saying she had enough family now to make up almost a whole town on their own.

Jessie just cocked her head to one side and looked at Jack. "Funny you should say that," she said. "We've been thinking on doing just that."

She looked up at the evening sky above us, thoughtful then, almost like she was having her own private talk with God. I saw her glance over at her children, and they all nodded, then Jessie looked back at us and smiled a smile that spoke of one that had run a long, hard race and had finally begun to just make out the finish line in the distance. "When we get the land to do it," Jessie said, almost like she was talking to herself, "we're gonna call it 'Justice.'"

"Well, I can't think of a finer name than that," Jack said softly. I looked over at Quinn, and we smiled at each other. I happened to look up then, and I saw that the stars had begun to come out, sprinkling the dusky sky with thousands of sparkling lights that seemed to hang so close over our heads that I felt I could almost touch them.

"Will you look at that?" I said, and everyone glanced upward, smiling, and I heard Jack suddenly speak something in Blackfoot to Medicine Weasel, heard them laugh.

"Hey, sis," Jack said, grinning mischievously. "Medicine Weasel says if you're ready for that crow, he's got a good recipe, says the way he makes it, it ain't so tough to chew."

Well, everyone laughed at that—even the children, who probably weren't so sure what they were laughing about but were just caught up in the joy of laughing. I was, too, and as I sat there, letting their laughter wash over me, I couldn't help thinking how funny life was. How God's answers to our prayers aren't ever what we expect them to be.

They're always better.

Acknowledgments

I TRULY BELIEVE the people God puts in our lives are for reasons far beyond what we could ever imagine. For writers, it's a true blessing to have friends and family who support them during the journey of writing a book. I couldn't imagine the journey of writing *Promiseland* without all of the dear people the Lord has put in my life. So these pages are for all of you who have been such shining examples of what family and friends are all about . . . what *love* is all about.

My cup runneth over . . .

To my family . . .

My son, Mitch: You are and will always be the "wind beneath my wings." I am so blessed to have you in my life, to laugh with, to love, to pray with . . . I thank God every day for blessing me with you. *My parents, Diana and Joe McClure,* whose witness brought me to the Lord: You have been there for me more times than I can count. Thank you for your love, for believing in me, and for all of your prayers. *My grandparents, Doug and Dorothy Vance:* You've always been there to listen when I needed to talk, to support me, to love me, and to make me laugh when I needed it the most . . . I love you all so very much . . .

To my friends . . .

Dawn Fansler, my prayer-warrior buddy and fellow author: Thank you so much for your help, for showing up at my door at just the right time—and for your friendship. *Shelly Guy:* Thank you so much for all your help, for your kind heart, and for all of our late-night chat sessions—they meant more than I can say. *Linda Glasford and Greg Johnson, my agents and friends at Alive Communications:* Thank you both so much for believing in me, for all your help and support—it's so wonderful to work with two such godly people. *Sue Ann Jones:* Thank you for being the best editor a girl could hope for. Your hard work and encouragement are appreciated. *David Moore:* Thank you for your prayers and your sincerity. God has great things in store for you! *Ann Pals:* you've been such a true friend and champion of Callie's story. Thank you, thank you, for always being there. *Joey Paul, publisher, Integrity Publishers:* Many thanks to you, Joey, for believing in *Promiseland* and for your patience and your true commitment to uplifting God in the written word. *Chelsea Perry:* Thank you so very much for praying, listening, for believing in my work, and for your calls that seemed to always come at just the right time. Our God *is* an awesome God. *Roy Quest,* fellow writer and friend, you are a true example of what it means to "walk the walk." Thank you so much for being there for me. *Terry Romeo:* Thanks for all your words of encouragement, for your prayers, and for your friendship. *Laurie and Joe White:* It seems as if we've known each other forever, and I am more than grateful for our friendship. You are the best of what true friends can be. I am so blessed!

To my pastors . . .
Jeff and Patsy Perry: I could fill more than one book on just what the two of you have done for me, for helping to

change my life in such a radical way through your messages of what it truly means to live a life for Jesus. I wish everyone could have the chance to witness what I have witnessed: to see such humbleness, grace, and love in action. You have made such a difference not only in my life but in my son's, and that means more to me than you will ever know . . . Thank you for being such an awesome inspiration in my life.

Pastor Don Henning: I can't thank you enough, Pastor Don, for your prayers and compassion. Your gentle spirit and giving heart are true gifts from God. *Pastor John Moore:* Thank you for your prayers and for your mentoring spirit; your legacy lives on in our children—and what a blessing that is for us all. *Pastor Virgil Nelson:* Thank you so much for your unwavering support, for your prayers, and for caring so much. *And for all the staff and members of St. Louis Family Church who are too numerous to mention:* I cherish you all; it is an honor to be a part of such a great group of people!

Finally, to all the dear readers who continue to take the time to write me such wonderful words of encouragement and praise—your letters have meant more to me than you will ever know.